The New York Times

IN THE HEADLINES

White Nationalists

WHO ARE THEY AND WHAT DO THEY BELIEVE?

EDUCATIONAL PUBLISHING BOOKS

THE NEW YORK TIMES EDITORIAL STAFF

Published in 2020 by New York Times Educational Publishing
in association with The Rosen Publishing Group, Inc.
29 East 21st Street, New York, NY 10010

First Edition

The New York Times
Alex Ward: Editorial Director, Book Development
Phyllis Collazo: Photo Rights/Permissions Editor
Heidi Giovine: Administrative Manager

Rosen Publishing
Megan Kellerman: Managing Editor
Julia Bosson: Editor
Greg Tucker: Creative Director
Brian Garvey: Art Director

Cataloging-in-Publication Data
Names: New York Times Company.
Title: White nationalists: who are they and what do they believe? / edited by the New York Times editorial staff.
Description: New York : New York Times Educational Publishing, 2020. | Series: In the headlines | Includes glossary and index.
Identifiers: ISBN 9781642822182 (library bound) | ISBN 9781642822175 (pbk.) | ISBN 9781642822199 (ebook)
Subjects: LCSH: White supremacy movements—United States—Juvenile literature. | Hate groups—United States—Juvenile literature. | Racism—Juvenile literature.
Classification: LCC E184.A1 W458 2020 | DDC 305.800973—dc23

Manufactured in the United States of America

On the cover: The statue of Confederate General Robert E. Lee stands behind a crowd of hundreds of white nationalists, neo-Nazis and members of the alt-right during the Unite the Right rally in Charlottesville, Va., Aug. 12, 2017; Chip Somodevilla/Getty Images.

Contents

CHAPTER 5

Charlottesville

Introduction

IN THE SUMMER of 2017, the college town of Charlottesville, Va., became embroiled in a debate over a statue of General Robert E. Lee, one of the many Confederate monuments in Southern cities that had been slated for removal. In response, a group of white nationalists organized a demonstration they called the "Unite the Right" rally. On Aug. 11, they descended on the town, holding torches and chanting "Blood and Soil" and "Jews will not replace us." The groups were met by police as well as counterprotesters, leading to violent altercations throughout the weekend that culminated in one white nationalist driving his car into a group of counterprotesters, killing a young woman.

The violence in Charlottesville gained national attention, filling the headlines of newspapers and dominating the conversation on news shows. Many Americans expressed shock, feeling taken aback at the idea that America might have such a prominent neo-Nazi presence so many years after the civil rights movement. This led journalists to investigate: Who are white nationalists? Where do they come from? What separates them from the Ku Klux Klan and other white supremacist groups? And what exactly do they believe?

The term "white nationalist" refers to a group of far-right activists who believe white people are superior to people of other races and who support racial segregation. White nationalists desire to create a white ethnostate that is built on common heritage and a white national identity. They adhere to theories of white racial superiority that have been entirely debunked by science, and see reports that America is on its way to becoming a white minority country as a sign of an impending race war that will require them to militarize for self-protection.

AL DRAGO FOR THE NEW YORK TIMES

White supremacists march toward Lafayette Square for the "Unite the Right" rally in Washington, Aug. 12, 2018, to mark the anniversary of their Charlottesville, Va. rally the previous year.

In recent years, white nationalists have made headlines following horrifyingly violent hate crimes. Dylann Roof, the young man who murdered nine parishioners at a historically black church in Charleston, S.C., was influenced by white nationalist rhetoric he encountered on online forums. Robert Bowers, the man who opened fire at the Tree of Life synagogue in Pittsburgh, Pa., taking the lives of nine, shared his views on Gab, a website that hosts forums for many fringe groups. White nationalism has become the greatest force of domestic terrorism today.

The leaders of the white nationalist movement represent the different strains of white supremacy present in American culture. There is Richard B. Spencer, the director of the National Policy Institute, who famously led an audience in a "Hail Trump!" salute following the 2016 election. There is David Duke, a former grand wizard of the Ku Klux Klan, who has made his own forays into politics. And then there is Don Black, the operator of the white nationalist website Stormfront.org, whose son, Derek Black, once his acolyte, made headlines by sharing his own conversion against white nationalism.

Part of the recent surge in white nationalism comes from the candidacy and election of Donald Trump. Throughout his campaign, Trump invoked the language of white nationalism, giving followers hope that his beliefs echoed theirs. He surrounded himself with advisers such as Steve Bannon, whose Breitbart News website gives a platform to the "alt-right," an association of extreme right-wing groups, including many white nationalists.

Those concerned about the spread of white nationalism found cause to worry after Charlottesville, when the president refrained from criticizing the alt-right groups, instead choosing to condemn the violence that took place "on both sides." Since then, the president has been slow to criticize racially motivated hate crimes and has put forward policy positions that echo the demands of white nationalists.

The articles in this book trace the origins of the white nationalist movement, examining its beliefs as well as its growing base of adherents. Reporters embedded themselves in white nationalist communities, scrutinized their means of operation and analyzed the foundations of their beliefs. What results is a portrait of how white nationalism has spread through national politics and how this has led to outbreaks of violence.

In 2018, protesters organized a second Unite the Right rally. Officials prepared themselves for a repeat of the previous year's violence, but the day passed peacefully, with counterprotesters greatly outnumbering the marching white nationalists. Whether this was a momentary setback or a sign of a shifting tide, only time will tell.

CHAPTER 1

White Nationalists and Their Beliefs

Who counts as a white nationalist, and what do they believe? White nationalism is a belief that sees whiteness as an ethnicity and seeks to create a white ethnostate in order to advance a white national identity. Built upon white supremacy and racism, white nationalists attempt to spread their beliefs through rallies, public talks and Internet platforms. As demographics shift and whites become a minority, white nationalists see the need to position themselves on the defensive, preparing for a race war.

White Supremacists Extend Their Reach Through Websites

BY MICHAEL WINES AND STEPHANIE SAUL | JULY 5, 2015

IN LATE JUNE, as much of the nation mourned the killing of nine parishioners in a Charleston, S.C., church, The Daily Stormer, a white supremacist website, was busy posting articles on a different issue: black crime against white people. "Adolescent Ape Jailed for Murdering White Man Out of Boredom," one headline blared.

And after Dylann Roof, a white 21-year-old high school dropout and the apparent author of a vitriolic anti-black diatribe, was arrested and charged with the killings, commenters on another white supremacist site, Stormfront.org, lamented something else: the possibility of the massacre's leading to gun control. "Jews want the white man's guns. End of story," one person wrote from Utah.

RYAN STONE FOR THE NEW YORK TIMES

Don Black, of Stormfront.org, was at one time a grand dragon of the Ku Klux Klan in Alabama. Now he does an Internet radio broadcast.

In the wake of the church massacre, many white supremacist groups have rushed to disavow any link to Mr. Roof and any role in the murders. And while Mr. Roof appears to have been in contact with some white supremacists online, investigators say it does not appear that those people encouraged or assisted in the deadly shootings.

Still, the authorities say, Mr. Roof had clearly embraced their worldview. As investigators comb through the data streams of Mr. Roof's electronic equipment, a four-page manifesto apparently written by him before the killings offers a virtual road map to modern-day white supremacy. It contains bitter complaints about black crime and immigration, espousing the virtues of segregation and debating the viability of an all-white enclave in the Pacific Northwest.

That manifesto has refocused attention on a shadowy movement that, for all its ideological connections to the white racists of the past, is more regionally diverse and sophisticated than its predecessors, experts say.

They say it is capable, through its robust online presence, of reaching an audience far wider than the small number of actual members attributed to it.

"There's really not a lot out there as far as membership organizations," said Don Black, who runs Stormfront.org. "But there is a huge number, I think more than ever, as far as people actively working in some way to promote our cause. Because they don't have to join an organization now that we have this newfangled Internet."

Experts dispute the number of movement supporters but agree about its efforts to modernize. While the virulent racism of old can still be found online, the movement today also includes more button-down websites run by white nationalism think tanks with vanity publishing units. Most of the best-known organizations also claim to have disavowed the violence of groups like the Ku Klux Klan.

Richard B. Spencer, the 37-year-old president of the white nationalist National Policy Institute in Whitefish, Mont., embodies this new generation.

He holds a master's degree from the University of Chicago and studied for a doctorate in history at Duke University. Now he runs an organization that produces papers on issues like racial differences in intelligence and the crime rate among Hispanic immigrants.

"America as it is currently constituted — and I don't just mean the government; I mean America as constituted spiritually and ideologically — is the fundamental problem," he said in an interview. "I don't support and agree with much of anything America is doing in the world."

But precisely because the movement is more atomized and has been rendered more anonymous by the Internet, law enforcement officials say it has become harder to track potentially violent lone-wolf terrorists who might draw inspiration from white supremacist sites without being actively involved in the organizations.

"White supremacist lone wolves pose the most significant domestic terrorist threat because of their low profile and autonomy — separate from any formalized group — which hampers warning efforts," said a Department of Homeland Security report issued in 2009. The report came under fierce criticism from conservatives, who said it unfairly painted them as terrorists.

If the movement has a leading edge, it is Stormfront.org, an online discussion forum. With about 40,000 visitors a day, it is perhaps the most popular supremacist site in the world based on page views, with more than a million a month (a figure that includes repeat visitors).

Mr. Black, its 61-year-old proprietor, straddles the movement's generational divide: a grand dragon of the Ku Klux Klan in Alabama decades ago, he later ushered in the movement's Internet era with Stormfront.org in 1995, and followed up with a two-hour weekday Internet radio show.

Stormfront's website, operated by Mr. Black out of his home in West Palm Beach, Fla., features the slogan "White Pride World Wide." It is primarily a chat room, with discussion threads that range from innocuous cooking tips to diatribes against gays, immigrants, Jews and blacks.

Mr. Black said he had broken from the Klan because it had a history of "random and senseless violence." But he also said he could not rule out violent conflict as white people tried to promote what he called "our heritage, our values," and attempted to realize the dream of a separate all-white enclave.

"I personally would like to see it play out peacefully," he said. "Unfortunately I took too many history classes, and history is not filled with a lot of peace. America is becoming balkanized just like the Balkans; we are breaking apart because of Hispanics — particularly in the Southwest — and other races."

Mr. Black was visited last week by F.B.I. agents seeking information about Mr. Roof's online associates, though he said there was no evidence that anybody had encouraged Mr. Roof to commit murder.

"This could obviously become overly broad and become a First Amendment issue," Mr. Black said, adding that such inquiries could have a chilling effect on free expression in online posts. He would not comment when asked if he had been served with a subpoena but said lawyers were involved.

A young challenger to Stormfront.org's influence is The Daily Stormer, a neo-Nazi mixture of message boards and sarcastic commentary begun by 30-year-old Andrew Anglin in 2013. He started it amid a national uproar over the killing in Florida of Trayvon Martin, an unarmed 17-year-old black youth, by a neighborhood watch monitor, George Zimmerman. Mr. Anglin was born in 1984. Like Mr. Black, he has a podcast.

The Daily Stormer offers frequently updated content, much of it provocatively raw and written by Mr. Anglin, who declined to be interviewed for this article but is believed to run the site out of suburban Columbus, Ohio. In a post on Friday headlined "Spineless Jewpublicans Respond to the Donald," Mr. Anglin took to task virtually the entire Republican presidential field for criticizing Donald Trump's statements on Mexican immigrants.

Several organizations — the National Policy Institute, American Renaissance, the Charles Martel Society and its website The Occidental Observer — try to take a more highbrow approach, couching white nationalist arguments as academic commentary on black inferiority, the immigration threat to whites and other racial issues.

There are also two prominent groups with deep ties to the South: the Council of Conservative Citizens, which evolved from the pro-segregationist White Citizens Councils, and the League of the South, a sparsely trafficked site for hard-core secessionists. The manifesto attributed to Mr. Roof cited the council's website as a source of information about black-on-white crime.

Many groups are said to be financially challenged. For instance, Stormfront.org struggles to raise $7,500 a month from about 800 "sustaining members" to cover expenses, Mr. Black said.

RYAN STONE FOR THE NEW YORK TIMES

Magnets on Mr. Black's refrigerator in West Palm Beach, Fla. Many adherents of the modern white supremacy movement have as a goal the restoration of white authority in America, or, if that proves impossible, the creation of a white enclave protected by its own army.

The exceptions are found among the highbrow organizations: The National Policy Institute and the Martel Society were founded and have been aided by William H. Regnery II, heir to a far-right publishing empire who also oversees a brace of anti-immigration lobbying groups. The Pioneer Fund, a 78-year-old nonprofit foundation that has stoked controversy with its interest in eugenics, also has aided the policy institute and American Renaissance.

In 2004, leaders of the movement met in New Orleans, ostensibly to celebrate the release of David Duke, the former grand wizard of the Ku Klux Klan, who had been imprisoned for fraudulent fund-raising. There, eight major organizations signed an agreement intended to define the modern supremacist movement according to three unifying principles: honorable behavior among all signatories, a high tone in public presentations and zero tolerance for violence.

The degree to which followers of those groups have maintained the nonviolence pledge remains in dispute.

But the manifesto attributed to Mr. Roof included a chilling complaint about the movement's disavowal of violence. "We have no skinheads, no real KKK, no one doing anything but talking on the Internet," the paper read. "Well, someone has to have the bravery to take it to the real world, and I guess that has to be me."

Supremacist groups remain divided by rivalries and philosophical disputes. Those differences sometimes obscure a common goal: to re-establish exclusive white control of the United States or, should that prove impossible as many groups now concede, to build an all-white enclave with its own government and an army to defend it.

The League of the South seeks a second Southern secession. The Daily Stormer's Mr. Anglin last month proposed building a white city, possibly in a foreign venue.

Mr. Spencer, who runs the National Policy Institute, said in an interview that he fantasized about an Aryan revival in the style of the Roman Empire. Others have proposed a white enclave in the Pacific Northwest, or "little Europe" towns across America.

Stormfront's Mr. Black does not just talk about such aspirations: He spent two years in federal prison for an ill-fated attempt in 1981 to seize the Caribbean island of Dominica for conversion into an all-white paradise, financed by brothels and casinos. The authorities stopped him and his group as they were boarding a yacht with plans to stage a Dominica coup.

Where the masses will be found to establish such audacious and widely condemned ventures is not clear, even to their proponents. But Mr. Spencer noted that Karl Marx had founded communism with no adherents and a simple manifesto. Mr. Black said he believed the online supremacist movement was not merely large but growing.

The Anti-Defamation League has identified some 10,000 white supremacists on websites and on social media like Facebook. But many more are said to be more like Mr. Roof, invisible and surfacing online only to make anonymous comments. Stormfront claims 300,000 registered members, although Mr. Black said only a small fraction were active on the site. Some 95 percent of the site's visitors, he said, are anonymous outsiders.

Among the dozen or so main white supremacist websites, daily page views range from fewer than 1,000 to as many as 40,000, although that figure includes repeat page views.

An analysis of traffic to several major supremacist websites shows that many attracted spikes in interest late last year, around the time that anger over the shooting of Michael Brown, an unarmed black teenager, by a white police officer in Ferguson, Mo., was touching off protests in cities and towns across the nation. But it remains far from clear whether it translated into a larger following for any of the groups.

Estimating the size of the white supremacy movement is "a murky guessing game," said Donald P. Green, a Columbia University professor and expert on hate crimes, because many racists are unwilling to declare a belief that mainstream Americans find abhorrent.

Gauging its impact on the Charleston murders, he said, is even harder.

"The idea that you could reaffirm someone's ideology and maybe even sharpen or focus it on a particular target is something these sites are capable of doing," Mr. Green said.

As for the church shooting suspect, Mr. Roof, "We don't know whether that was a marker for his violent predispositions or might be the cause of them," Mr. Green said. "It might be both."

SAMARTH BHASKAR contributed reporting.

‘White Nationalism,’ Explained

BY AMANDA TAUB | NOV. 21, 2016

A QUESTION HAS BEEN posed in a puzzled whisper in many of the nation’s living rooms and newsrooms ever since Donald J. Trump’s triumph in this month’s presidential election: What, exactly, is white nationalism?

Self-proclaimed white nationalists have happily embraced Mr. Trump’s victory and, particularly, his choice of Stephen K. Bannon as chief strategist, as a win for their agenda. A barrage of groups that fight discrimination and hate speech have, in turn, criticized Mr. Bannon’s appointment, warning that his embrace of the “alt-right” movement was little more than an attempt to rebrand racism and white nationalism into something palatable enough for mass consumption.

And much of the rest of the country has been left to wonder what this unfamiliar term actually means.

While white nationalism certainly overlaps with white supremacy and racism, many political scientists say it is a distinct phenomenon — one that was a powerful but often-unseen force during the presidential election and will most likely remain a potent factor in American and European politics in coming years.

Eric Kaufmann, a professor of politics at Birkbeck University in London, has spent years studying the ways that ethnicity intersects with politics. While most researchers in that field focus on ethnic minorities, Professor Kaufmann does the opposite: He studies the behavior of ethnic majorities, particularly whites in the United States and Britain.

White nationalism, he said, is the belief that national identity should be built around white ethnicity, and that white people should therefore maintain both a demographic majority and dominance of the nation’s culture and public life.

So, like white supremacy, white nationalism places the interests of white people over those of other racial groups. White supremacists and white nationalists both believe that racial discrimination should be incorporated into law and policy.

Some will see the distinction between white nationalism and white supremacy as a semantic sleight of hand. But although many white supremacists are also white nationalists, and vice versa, Professor Kaufmann says the terms are not synonyms: White supremacy is based on a racist belief that white people are innately superior to people of other races; white nationalism is about maintaining political and economic dominance, not just a numerical majority or cultural hegemony.

For a long time, he said, white nationalism was less an ideology than the default presumption of American life. Until quite recently, white Americans could easily see the nation as essentially an extension of their own ethnic group.

But the country's changing demographics, the civil rights movement and a push for multiculturalism in many quarters mean that white Americans are now confronting the prospect of a nation that is no longer built solely around their own identity.

For many white people, of course, the growing diversity is something to celebrate. But for others it is a source of stress. The white nationalist movement has drawn support from that latter group. Its supporters argue that the United States should protect its white majority by sharply limiting immigration, and perhaps even by compelling nonwhite citizens to leave.

Mr. Trump's appointment of Mr. Bannon as his senior counselor and chief West Wing strategist has, more than anything, brought white nationalism to the forefront of conversation. He is the former editor of Breitbart News, a site he described in August to Mother Jones as "the platform of the alt-right." Although the alt-right is ideologically broader than white nationalism — it also includes neoreactionaries, monarchists and meme-loving internet trolls — white nationalism makes up a significant part of its appeal.

For instance, Richard B. Spencer, who runs the website AlternativeRight.com, is also the director of the National Policy

Institute, an organization that says it is devoted to protecting the "heritage, identity, and future of people of European descent in the United States, and around the world."

Mr. Spencer argues that immigration and multiculturalism are threats to America's white population, and has said his ideal is a white "ethno-state." He has avoided discussing the details of how this might be achieved, saying it is still just a "dream," but has called for "peaceful ethnic cleansing" to remove nonwhite people from American soil.

Mr. Bannon, the Trump adviser, told The New York Times upon his appointment that he does not share those ethno-nationalist views. But under his leadership, Breitbart News has gone to considerable lengths to cater to an audience that does. And in a 2015 radio interview that was resurfaced this week by The Washington Post, Mr. Bannon opposed even highly skilled immigration, implying he believed it was a threat to American culture.

"When two-thirds or three-quarters of the C.E.O.s in Silicon Valley are from South Asia or from Asia, I think ...," he said, trailing off mid-sentence before continuing a moment later, "a country is more than an economy. We're a civic society."

White nationalists, including Mr. Spencer, have rejoiced at Mr. Bannon's appointment to such a senior position in the Trump White House. But focusing on high-profile figures like Mr. Bannon may obscure the more significant way that white nationalist ideas are affecting politics — and fueling the rise of politicians like Mr. Trump in the United States as well as anti-immigrant populist movements in Britain and continental Europe.

Several studies of other countries have found that a desire to protect traditional values and culture is the strongest predictor of support for the sort of populism that propelled Mr. Trump to power in the United States.

Many of those voters would not think of themselves as white nationalists, and the cultural values and traditions they seek to protect are not necessarily explicitly racial. However, those traditions formed when national identity and culture were essentially synonymous with whiteness. So the impulse to protect them from social and demographic change is essentially an attempt to turn back the clock to a less-diverse time.

A recent working paper by Pippa Norris, a political scientist at Harvard's Kennedy School of Government, and Ronald Inglehart, a political scientist at the University of Michigan, concluded, based on an analysis of wide-ranging survey data, that populists have succeeded by appealing to the cultural anxiety of groups like older white men, who once formed the cultural majority in Western societies "but have recently seen their predominance and privilege eroded."

Elisabeth Ivarsflaten, a professor of politics at the University of Bergen in Norway, came to a similar conclusion after studying anti-immigrant policies in Europe. Their supporters, she found, were motivated by a desire to protect their national culture — suggesting they believed that immigrants posed a threat to it.

Mr. Trump's criticism of immigrants and promise to "make America great again" may have tapped into those same cultural anxieties, fueling his success with older and less-educated white voters. (Over all, he won white voters by 21 percentage points.)

Professor Kaufmann argues that anxiety over white identity and anti-immigrant populist politicians can have a symbiotic relationship, each strengthening the other. When populist politicians gain mainstream success, that can make white nationalist ideas more socially acceptable.

"It's not just a question of ethnic change and people being alarmed over it," he said. "It's also a question of what people see as the boundaries of acceptable opposition. It's about what counts as racism, and whether it's racist to vote for a far-right party."

"This is all about the anti-racist norm," Professor Kaufmann continued. "If it's weakening or eroding because people think the boundaries have shifted."

What White Nationalism Gets Right About American History

OPINION | BY R. DEREK BLACK | AUG. 19, 2017

MY DAD OFTEN gave me the advice that white nationalists are not looking to recruit people on the fringes of American culture, but rather the people who start a sentence by saying, "I'm not racist, but ..."

The most effective tactics for white nationalists are to associate American history with themselves and to suggest that the collective efforts to turn away from our white supremacist past are the same as abandoning American culture. My father, the founder of the white nationalist website Stormfront, knew this well. It's a message that erases people of color and their essential role in American life, but one that also appeals to large numbers of white people who would agree with the statement, "I'm not racist, but I don't want American history dishonored, and this statue of Robert E. Lee shouldn't be removed."

I was raised by the leaders of the white nationalist movement with a model of American history that described a vigorous white supremacist past and once again I find myself observing events in which I once might have participated before I rejected the white nationalist cause several years ago. After the dramatic, horrible and rightly unnerving events in Charlottesville, Va., this past weekend, I had to make separate calls: one to make sure no one in my family who might have attended the rally got hurt, and a second to see if any friends at the University of Virginia had been injured in the crowd of counterprotesters.

On Tuesday afternoon the president defended the actions of those at the rally, stating, "You also had people that were very fine people, on both sides." His words marked possibly the most important moment in the history of the modern white nationalist movement. These statements described the marchers as they see themselves — nobly driven

ILLUSTRATION BY MATTHIEU BOUREL, PHOTOGRAPH BY EDU BAYER FOR THE NEW YORK TIMES

by a good cause, even if they are plagued by a few bad apples. He said: "I'm not talking about the neo-Nazis and the white nationalists, because they should be condemned totally. But you had many people in that group other than neo-Nazis and white nationalists."

But this protest, contrary to his defense, was advertised unambiguously as a white nationalist rally. The marchers chanted, "Jews will not replace us"; in the days leading up to the event, its organizers called it "a pro-white demonstration"; my godfather, David Duke, attended and said it was meant to "fulfill the promises of Donald Trump"; and many attendees flew swastika flags. Whatever else you might say about the rally, they were not trying to deceive anyone.

Almost by definition, the white nationalist movement over the past 40 years has worked against the political establishment. It was too easy for politicians to condemn the movement — even when there was overlap on policy issues — because it was a liability without enough political force to make the huge cost of associating with it worthwhile. Until Tuesday, I didn't believe that had changed.

We have all observed the administration's decisions over the past several months that aligned with the white nationalist agenda, such as limiting or completely cutting off legal and illegal immigration, especially of Hispanics and Muslims; denigrating black communities as criminal and poor, threatening to unleash an even greater police force on them; and going after affirmative action as antiwhite discrimination. But I had never believed Trump's administration would have trouble distancing itself from the actual white nationalist movement.

Yet President Trump stepped in to salvage the message that the rally organizers had originally hoped to project: "George Washington was a slave owner," he said, and asked, "So will George Washington now lose his status?" Then: "How about Thomas Jefferson?" he asked. "Because he was a major slave owner. Now are we going to take down his statue?" He added: "You're changing history. You're changing culture."

Until Trump's comments, few critics seemed to identify the larger relationship the alt-right sees between its beliefs and the ideals of the American founders. Charlottesville is synonymous with Jefferson. The city lies at the foot of Monticello and is the home of the University of Virginia, the school he founded. Over the years I've made several pilgrimages to Charlottesville, both when I was a white nationalist and since I renounced the ideology. While we all know that Jefferson was the author of the Declaration of Independence, which declared that "all men are created equal," his writings also offer room for explicitly white nationalist interpretation.

My father observed many times that the quotation from Jefferson's autobiography embedded on the Jefferson Memorial is deceptive because it reads, "Nothing is more certainly written in the book of fate than that these [the Negro] people are to be free." It does not include the second half of the sentence: "Nor is it less certain that the two races, equally free, cannot live in the same government. Nature, habit, opinion has drawn indelible lines of distinction between them."

Jefferson's writings partly inspired the American colonization movement, which encouraged the return of free black people to

Africa — a goal that was pursued even by Abraham Lincoln during the first years of the Civil War.

The most fundamental legislative goal of the white nationalist movement is to limit nonwhite immigration. It is important to remember that such limits were in place during the lifetimes of many current white nationalists; it was the default status until the 1960s. In the 1790s, the first naturalization laws of the United States Congress limited citizenship to a "free white person."

Legislation in the 1920s created quotas for immigration based on national origin, which placed severe restrictions on the total number of immigrants and favored northern and western European immigration. It was only with the civil rights movement of the 1960s that the national origin quota system was abolished and Congress fully removed the restriction favoring white immigrants.

I'm not offering these historical anecdotes to defame the history of the country. I'm not calling for Jefferson's statue to be removed along with the Confederate memorials. I do, however, think it is essential that we recognize that the white nationalist history embedded in American culture lends itself to white nationalist rallies like the one in Charlottesville. If you want to preserve Confederate memorials, but you don't work to build monuments to historical black leaders, you share the same cause as the marchers.

Until Tuesday I believed the organizers of the rally had failed in their goal to make their movement more appealing to average white Americans. The rally superimposed Jefferson's image on that of a pseudo K.K.K. rally and brought the overlap between Jefferson and white nationalist ideas to mind for anyone looking to find them. But the horrific violence that followed seemed to hurt their cause.

And then President Trump intervened. His comments supporting the rally gave new purpose to the white nationalist movement, unlike any endorsement it has ever received. Among its followers, being at that rally will become something to brag about, and some people who didn't want to be associated with extremism will now see the cause as more mainstream. When the president doesn't provide condemnation that he has been pressed to give, what message does that send but encouragement?

The United States was founded as a white nationalist country, and that legacy remains today. Things have improved from the radical promotion of white people at the expense of all others, which has persisted for most of our history, yet most of us have not accepted the extent to which white identity guides so much of what we still do. Sometimes it seems that the white nationalists are most honest about the very real foundation of white supremacy upon which our nation was built.

The president's words legitimized the worst of our country, and now the white nationalist movement could be poised to grow. To challenge these messages, we need to acknowledge the continuity of white nationalist thought in American history, and the appeal it still holds.

It is a fringe movement not because its ideas are completely alien to our culture, but because we work constantly to argue against it, expose its inconsistencies and persuade our citizens to counter it. We can no longer count on the country's leader to do this, so it's now incumbent upon all of us.

R. DEREK BLACK is a graduate student in history, focusing on the early Middle Ages.

Rhodesia's Dead — but White Supremacists Have Given It New Life Online

BY JOHN ISMAY | APRIL 10, 2018

IN THE SEPIA-TONED PHOTO, two white soldiers patrol on foot over brush and rocky ground. Lean and bearded, they carry what appear to be Belgian rifles, and they wear an unusual uniform — cloth jungle hats, short shorts and tennis shoes — associated with a military unit that was disbanded nearly 40 years ago.

That unit was called the Selous Scouts, a special-forces regiment from the Rhodesian Army, which fought black insurgent armies in the Bush War of the 1960s and '70s to maintain white-minority rule over territory that is now Zimbabwe.

Not long after Rhodesia ceased to exist, it became morally untenable to mourn its disappearance. As the rest of the world woke up to the injustices of Western colonialism and its system of white-minority governments, the Selous Scouts and their cause became taboo.

But late last year, the image of two Scouts began to circulate on Instagram, part of a social-media resurgence of Rhodesia as a source of inspiration. Photos of soldiers marching through grassland and rivers, special-forces units jumping out of helicopters and civilians posing in front of their homes with rifles collected hundreds, sometimes thousands, of likes on posts seeming to offer tribute to a hardened and forgotten cadre of Cold War-era bush fighters. The online movement also caught the attention of opportunistic apparel marketers who started selling Rhodesian-themed T-shirts, posters and patches, among other collectibles.

Nostalgia for Rhodesia has since grown into a subtle and profitable form of racist messaging, with its own line of terminology, hashtags and merchandise, peddled to military-history fans and firearms enthusiasts by a stew of far-right provocateurs.

In conversations and email exchanges with The New York Times, some prominent social-media figures and companies selling Rhodesia-themed merchandise denied trafficking in white-power messages, or said they had done so unwittingly. A few said their affinity for Rhodesia derived from the government's supposed anti-communist stance.

But outside observers of this Rhodesia revival cite a far more disturbing inspiration for it: Dylann Roof, the American white supremacist who killed nine black parishioners in a Charleston, S.C., church in June 2015. Roof, who was sentenced to death last year, had penned an online manifesto, which appeared on a website called The Last Rhodesian, with photographs of himself wearing a jacket with a patch of the green-and-white Rhodesian flag.

Demand for Rhodesian-themed apparel has since increased. Today one retailer, the Commissar Clothing Company, offers "Make Zimbabwe Rhodesia Again" hoodies and T-shirts and others that read "Be a Man Among Men," a Rhodesian Army recruiting slogan now used by hate groups. The online store was taken down in March, but its merchandise is still available on the company's eBay storefront.

Another retailer of Rhodesia-themed goods, the Western Outlands Supply Company, which is listed by the Southern Poverty Law Center as a "white nationalist hate group," was formerly known as Right Wing Death Squad and sold similar fare, in addition to apparel featuring Crusader crosses and medieval symbols like those seen at the Charlottesville "Unite the Right" rally last year.

Commissar goes further, offering shirts that say "Slot Floppies," a phrase that is sometimes used as a hashtag on Instagram and other social media platforms to promote Rhodesian-themed posts and messaging. "Floppy," in 1970s Rhodesia, was the equivalent of an unprintable racist epithet in the United States, while "slot" was Rhodesian military slang for "shoot."

When The Times asked Instagram whether #MakeZimbabwe-RhodesiaAgain and other hashtags violated community standards, the social-media company issued this statement: "We have blocked these hashtags for violating our hate-speech policies," it said, "and they will no longer be searchable on Instagram."

If such symbols and slogans, for a North American audience, lack the instant shock effect of a Confederate or Nazi flag, that is part of the point. Commissar Clothing's website, now shuttered, explained its products' wink-and-nod appeal: "We think you should be able to tell the world about you without saying a word," it read. "The great thing about most of our designs is that they are essentially inside jokes and references that the general public will not understand."

When reached by email, Commissar Clothing's owner, Alexander Smyth, said, "I do not support or condone racism of any sort."

The online apparel company FireForce Ventures, whose website is registered to the Canadian Army reservist Henry Lung, offers reproduction Rhodesian flags, recruiting posters and various patches of the Rhodesian security forces. Lung, who is of Chinese descent, told The Times, "I see the veteran community, the Rhodesian community, as one to be honored," but insisted that he was not a white supremacist, and that he was "just trying to make a little bit of extra cash."

Heidi Beirich, head of the Southern Poverty Law Center's Intelligence Project, said the uptick of pro-Rhodesian messaging is a purposeful amplification of the ideology and practice of "racist colonial regimes" — and possibly even an exhortation to war.

"All the talk right now among people in the alt-right and the broader white supremacist movement is about the need for a white ethno-state," she said. "And when you praise Rhodesia, in this context, what you're praising is violence to that end."

"There were no defenses for apartheid regimes and colonialism 20 years ago," Beirich added. "And now all of a sudden we're seeing this stuff pop up."

Southern Rhodesia was established in 1923 as a British colony named for Cecil Rhodes, who made his fortune in consolidating diamond mines. By the 1960s, as much of Africa rapidly decolonized around it, the colonial government faced pressure from London to hold free elections and accede to majority rule.

The colonial government refused. In 1965 it renamed itself Rhodesia and broke from the United Kingdom with the express purpose of maintaining white rule. The new government was led by Ian Smith, who declared that "the white man is master of Rhodesia. He has built it, and he intends to keep it."

Smith's government soon found itself at war with a black insurgency, fighting for representative government and self-rule. Many of the fighters received weapons from China or the Soviet Union. Rhodesia's government labeled them "communists" and "terrorists."

"It's a complicated story," said Gerald Horne, author of "From the Barrel of a Gun" and a professor of history and African-American studies at the University of Houston. "But of course the apartheid side knew what sold in Washington, so they portrayed it as a battle against communism because it got pulses racing in the United States."

The battle for perception is playing out again now on social media, which pro-Rhodesia accounts or commenters are using to rewrite Rhodesian history in gentle tones. On Jan. 27, the Instagram page @historicalwarfareinc posted a photo, claiming it depicted an army officer deciding the fate of a prisoner.

The photograph is well known. It was taken in September 1977 by an Associated Press photographer, J. Ross Baughman, who was awarded a Pulitzer Prize for capturing the brutality of the Rhodesian Army.

That Instagram caption provides far less context than the version submitted for the Pulitzer, which read: "Lt. Graham Baillie raps a small wooden bat against his leg after using it to beat Moffat Ncube, a local teacher, political leader and now a bound, unconscious prisoner slumped against the wall of schoolhouse, 20 September 1977."

It added: "Ncube reportedly later died after three days of brutal, nonstop torture."

As of April 6, the photo with the more anodyne caption had nearly 1,850 likes.

Some pro-Rhodesia voices on social media are not so subtle.

Last December Joseph Smith, a 22-year-old resident of Rexburg, Idaho, who told The Times he had not heard of Rhodesia until 18 months ago, posted a YouTube video that he said offered "a quick rundown" of Rhodesian history. The video has received more than 180,000 views.

Comments on it included calls for Rhodesia to return, claims that the West betrayed Rhodesia and outright hostility to the idea of black-majority rule. With more than 1,700 comments in just the last three months, the discussion quickly devolved into a stream of racial and ethnic slurs against African-Americans and Jews, calling for them to be shoved into gas chambers and ovens.

In an email to The Times, Smith wrote that he felt persecuted and that he has found Rhodesian themes compelling. "I'm sure you're aware these days being a conservative heterosexual white male is rather unpopular in the eyes of many," and that "this is the demographic that caused Rhodesia to thrive as well as it did for as long as it did."

He insisted, however, that his attraction to Rhodesian nostalgia was not racist. "I do not think that it's a race issue though," he wrote. "Partly I just feel like white people like having a team to root for these days."

An examination of retailers and social-media accounts showed a varied understanding and mixed approaches to addressing the meanings in the pro-Rhodesia messaging.

The Selous Armory, a Massachusetts apparel company run by Sean Lucht, a Boston firefighter and Marine veteran, sold a red-and-white "Make Zimbabwe Rhodesia Again" patch online until recently. The site also sold T-shirts with sayings like "Rhodesians Never Die" and "Apply Violence" with the Rhodesian Foreign Legion logo, in addition to "Be a Man Among Men" posters. When The Times reached out to

Lucht for comment about the business in March, all the merchandise was stripped from the website and an announcement was published on its home page saying, "The Selous Armory was always a place for military history/humor and never a place for hate." The announcement added that the Selous Armory had ceased all operations. Lucht did not respond to numerous requests for comment.

The Instagram account of retired Delta Force master sergeant Larry Vickers also displays an affinity for Rhodesia.

With roughly 900,000 followers on YouTube, Facebook and Instagram, Vickers — a marksmanship instructor who says he trains special-operations forces, law enforcement and civilians — attracts a social-media audience with an interest in military history and firearms.

On Instagram, Vickers first publicly professed his fondness for Rhodesian history in September 2014, posting a photo of Rhodesian soldiers returning from a raid. Since 2017, he has shared many photos of Belgian FAL rifles painted in the splotchy yellow-and-green camouflage favored by Rhodesian troops in the Bush War of the 1970s.

The caption on one photo from last year expressed reverence: "Respect and remember," it read. In a telephone interview, Vickers told The Times that his attraction to the Rhodesian security forces stems from their having carried out "some of the most daring special operations missions in history on a shoestring." He has repeatedly referred to the fall of Rhodesia as "the greatest tragedy of the post-World War II era." His own YouTube videos on the Rhodesian rifle have nearly 300,000 page views. Racist comments and calls for racist violence cluttered the comments sections — until he was asked about them by The Times.

Vickers said he was unaware of the comments, and has since turned the comments function on some videos off. On March 16, he went a step further and issued a public rebuke on his Facebook page, saying, "Everyone is entitled to their opinion, but if your opinion is racist and demeaning you can go elsewhere as that is not welcome here."

It appears that he has not deleted any of his Instagram posts mentioning Rhodesia.

Vickers's apparent concern was shared by the owner of DS Arms, an Illinois-based firearms manufacturer, which, in March, wrote on Instagram that it will be releasing a "Rhodie tribute rifle" along with T-shirts featuring the "Be a Man Among Men" Rhodesian recruiting insignia. DS Arms also sells a challenge coin embossed with the same emblem.

The owner of the company, David Selvaggio, said in a telephone interview that he did not know what had been driving recent online interest in Rhodesia. "I've been told that yes, there's young guys getting into it and they're showing an interest in it. I'm not sure why."

When told that the Rhodesian rifle had become a totem for American white supremacists, Selvaggio pleaded ignorance. "What I remember of it is seeing pictures of the FALs on the guys over there fighting. I don't even know what they were fighting, except against communism, from what I was told. Maybe I need to do some studying on my history here."

He added that he hoped the next Dylann Roof wouldn't carry one of his company's rifles. "That does concern me," he said. "I don't want anybody saying, 'Hey, this is a call to arms, and we have to use a FAL, and we're for this crazy wacko group.' That's not us."

For Beirich, it's impossible to pay tribute to the Rhodesian security forces and their equipment without also glorifying the ideology the country was built on.

"In the same way you don't have people glorifying Nazi soldiers without understanding what the regime fought for," Beirich said. "You can't separate fighting for the Confederacy from the ultimate goal of the Confederacy."

JOHN ISMAY covers armed conflict for The New York Times Magazine out of Washington.

The Housewives of White Supremacy

OPINION | BY ANNIE KELLY | JUNE 1, 2018

IN A PODCAST INTERVIEW posted last spring, Nicole Jorgenson, a singer and former schoolteacher in North Dakota, explains to her host that she has never been happier since marrying and having children. And yet between cute pastoral anecdotes of growing her own vegetables and making banana bread, it soon becomes clear that Ms. Jorgenson is advocating something sinister — not just a return to agrarian motherhood.

She lived in Germany temporarily, she says, but left just before "an influx of refugees took over the country." She just had a child and thinks the new baby is beautiful — but maybe not quite in the same way all mothers do: "I always wanted children that looked like me," she says, "blond-haired, blue-eyed babies, but I kind of had to say it under my breath."

By the time the interviewer begins to gush about how wonderful it is that Ms. Jorgenson and her husband are both of Norwegian heritage — "you guys come from the same blood" — it's clear what political demographic both women are catering to. Ms. Jorgenson is being interviewed on Radio 3Fourteen, a white supremacist talk radio program; it is interviewing her because she considers herself a tradwife.

The digital far right, frequently called the alt-right, is largely regarded as a men-only space. The photographs from the white nationalist rally in Charlottesville, Va., were striking for the lack of female faces in a sea of button-down-wearing snarls. The movement shares DNA with so-called incels, a network of men who feel women have unfairly denied them sexual relationships. And it is defined in part by its misogyny and its anti-feminist, anti-woman language.

But some members of the alt-right have been weighing whether the absence of women from their movement is a problem. In 2016, the Swedish nationalist Marcus Follin, who calls himself The Golden One on YouTube, made a video titled "The Women Question." In it, he urged his followers to dial down the open misogyny and consider new strategies to win over more women to the white nationalist cause. Mr. Follin was responding to statistics from the Austrian presidential election that year, in which female voters helped swing the election away from the candidate of the far-right Freedom Party. "You might not like that women have the right to vote, you might not like that anyone has the right to vote," Mr. Follin conceded, "but it's about winning a long-term political victory."

Enter the tradwives.

Over the past few years, dozens of YouTube and social media accounts have sprung up showcasing soft-spoken young white women who extol the virtues of staying at home, submitting to male leadership and bearing lots of children — being "traditional wives." These accounts pepper their messages with scrapbook-style collections of 1950s advertising images showing glamorous mothers in lipstick and heels with happy families and beautiful, opulent homes. They give their videos titles like "Female Nature and Advice for Young Ladies," "How I Homeschool" and "You Might be a Millennial Housewife If...."

But running alongside what could be mistaken for a peculiar style of mommy-vlogging is a virulent strain of white nationalism. One such advocate who calls herself "Wife With a Purpose" made international headlines last year when she issued something she titled "the white baby challenge." Citing falling white birthrates in the West, she urged her followers to procreate. "I've made six!" she wrote. "Match or beat me!" Wife With a Purpose might be the most prominent and certainly most openly white supremacist of the women who call themselves tradwives, but she is not an anomaly: These accounts veer dizzyingly from Cosmo-style tips on pleasing your husband to racist musings about "ghetto music" to, on some occasions, calls to reassert their vision of the white race. The seemingly anachronistic way they dress is no accident. The deliberately hyperfeminine aesthetics are constructed precisely to mask the authoritarianism of their ideology.

There is nothing particularly new about this message within the far right. And tradwives still constitute a niche digital subculture. There's a clear market for their message — the biggest tradwife accounts usually surge to about 10,000 YouTube subscribers in just a year of posting — but their male alt-right counterparts have 10 times the number of followers.

Still, tradwives remain worth contemplating because they help illuminate some of the forces that drive the alt-right and where the movement might be going. The alt-right is abhorrent; it is racist and hate-filled. But it is, like any other mass movement, also driven by a sense of dissatisfaction with modern life. Tradwives help us understand the sources of that dissatisfaction by revealing points of overlap between red-lipsticked mothers of six and the men who complain of being "kissless virgins."

A frustrated yearning for a mythic past of material abundance, at a time when it is becoming increasingly difficult for young people to build careers and achieve financial security, is not gender-specific. Young people face ever more obstacles, higher demands and continually dwindling returns in the form of work benefits, job security and pay. We shouldn't underestimate how some young white women, when faced with this bleak economic landscape and then presented with a rosy image of 1950s domestic bliss, may look back to 1960s Friedan-era feminism as having cheated them out of a family and a luxurious lifestyle, all supported by a single income. The men on the alt-right might point to diversity initiatives and mass immigration as having dismantled their career prospects; the women are furious that they have to consider career prospects at all.

Tradwives also point to the ways that the half-finished work of the sexual revolution has brought about not just male but also female discontents. The likes of pickup artists and incels claim that the sexual revolution has brought about a consequence-free life of pleasure for young women, while socially awkward or unattractive men are left behind. But the existence of tradwives points to a more nuanced reality. Female fears of objectification and sexual violence remain as potent as ever; the tradwife subculture exploits them by blaming modernity for such phenomena, and then offers chastity, marriage and motherhood as an escape. As one such YouTube commentator, a teenager, told her audience, traditionalism does "what feminism is supposed to do" in preventing women from being made into "sexual objects" and treated "like a whore."

It's a lie, of course. Modesty has never been a safeguard against degradation or rape, and we know that a rapist is no less likely to hurt a woman simply because he's married to her. But it's not difficult to see how it could be a seductive lie; the continuous headlines made by the #MeToo movement, paradoxically, were eagerly shared among tradwife networks, as supposed proof that sexual liberation had made life unacceptably dangerous for women.

At present, these shared dissatisfactions haven't helped the alt-right recruit significant numbers of women because, quite simply, the men cannot keep their seething misogyny in check. Women, even those initially sympathetic to alt-right ideas, face blistering hostility on alt-right message boards and forums when they try to participate. Several longtime alt-right commentators have begun to post lengthy warnings denouncing " trad thots" — women they deem disingenuous in their support — who they say latch onto the movement as a source of fame or money. Lauren Southern, an alt-right YouTube commentator, recently put out a video called "Why I'm Not Married," in which she pleaded with her audience to stop calling her a "degenerate" for not being married with children at age 22. It's exceedingly difficult to feel sorry for Ms. Southern, whose stunts have included attempting to block direly needed refugee rescue boats off the coast of Italy. But it's understandable that even women with white nationalist sympathies may not be leaping to sign up for this kind of treatment.

Like most political networks primarily based on the internet, the alt-right evolved extremely fast. When I began studying digital anti-feminist and far-right networks for my doctorate in 2015, the number of women in these spaces seemed small enough to be insignificant.

There has since been such a surfeit of women beginning careers off such networks, many infusing their particular brand of far-right ideology with "trad" rhetoric, that it now seems irresponsible not to think about them, their roles and what they reveal. The material conditions that allow far-right movements to thrive seem unlikely to change, and feminism's work is far from done in countering the kind of sexual anxieties that the alt-right exploits. Tradwives may seem like a lunatic fringe at present, but they may not stay one for long.

ANNIE KELLY is a Ph.D. student at the University of East Anglia researching the impact of digital cultures on anti-feminism and the far-right.

Why White Supremacists Are Chugging Milk (and Why Geneticists Are Alarmed)

BY AMY HARMON | OCT. 17, 2018

NOWHERE ON THE AGENDA of the annual meeting of the American Society of Human Genetics, being held in San Diego this week, is a topic plaguing many of its members: the recurring appropriation of the field's research in the name of white supremacy.

"Sticking your neck out on political issues is difficult," said Jennifer Wagner, a bioethicist and president of the group's social issues committee, who had sought to convene a panel on the racist misuse of genetics and found little traction.

But the specter of the field's ignominious past, which includes support for the American eugenics movement, looms large for many geneticists in light of today's white identity politics. They also worry about how new tools that are allowing them to home in on the genetic basis of hot-button traits like intelligence will be misconstrued to fit racist ideologies.

In recent months, some scientists have spotted distortions of their own academic papers in far-right internet forums. Others have fielded confused queries about claims of white superiority wrapped in the jargon of human genetics. Misconceptions about how genes factor into America's stark racial disparities have surfaced in the nation's increasingly heated arguments over school achievement gaps, immigration and policing.

Instead of long-discounted proxies like skull circumference and family pedigrees, according to experts who track the far-right, today's proponents of racial hierarchy are making their case by misinterpreting research on the human genome itself. And in debates that have largely been limited to ivory-tower forums, the scientists whose job is to mine humanity's genetic variations for the collective good are grappling with how to respond.

"Studying human genetic diversity is easier in a society where diversity is clearly valued and celebrated — right now, that is very much on my mind," said John Novembre, a University of Chicago evolutionary biologist who has taken to concluding his visiting seminars by illustrating how one of the field's textbook examples of natural selection has been adopted for illiberal ends.

One slide Dr. Novembre has folded into his recent talks depicts a group of white nationalists chugging milk at a 2017 gathering to draw attention to a genetic trait known to be more common in white people than others — the ability to digest lactose as adults. It also shows a social media post from an account called "Enter The Milk Zone" with a map lifted from a scientific journal article on the trait's evolutionary history.

In most of the world, the article explains, the gene that allows for the digestion of lactose switches off after childhood. But with the arrival of the first cattle herders in Europe some 5,000 years ago, a chance mutation that left it turned on provided enough of a nutritional leg up that nearly all of those who survived eventually carried it. In the post, the link is accompanied by a snippet of hate speech urging individuals of African ancestry to leave America. "If you can't drink milk," it says in part, "you have to go back."

In an inconvenient truth for white supremacists, a similar bit of evolution turns out to have occurred among cattle breeders in East Africa. Scientists need to be more aware of the racial lens through which some of their basic findings are being filtered, Dr. Novembre says, and do a better job at pointing out how they can be twisted.

But the white nationalist infatuation with dairy also heightened Dr. Novembre's concerns about how to handle new evolutionary studies that deal with behavioral traits, such as how long people stay in school.

Anticipating misinterpretations of a recent study on how genes associated with high education attainment, identified in Europeans, varied in different populations around the world, the lead author, Fernando Racimo, created his own "frequently asked questions" document for nonscientists, which he posted on Twitter.

And in a commentary that accompanied the paper in the journal Genetics, Dr. Novembre warned that such research is "wrapped in numerous caveats" that are likely to get lost in translation.

"Great care," his commentary concludes, "should be taken in communicating results of these studies to general audiences."

Already, some of those audiences are flaunting DNA ancestry test results indicating exclusively European heritage as though they were racial ID cards. They are celebrating traces of Neanderthal DNA not found in people with only African ancestry. And they are trading messages with the coded term "race realism," which takes oxygen from the claim that the liberal scientific establishment has obscured the truth about biological racial differences.

Some scientists suggest that engaging with racists would simply lend credibility to obviously specious claims. Many say that they do not study race, in any case: The racial categories used by the United States census correlate only imperfectly with the geographic ancestry groupings of interest to evolutionary geneticists. "Black," for instance, is a socially defined term that includes many Americans who have a majority of European ancestry.

But as the pace of human population genetics research has accelerated, it has yielded results that, to many nonscientists, appear to challenge the idea of race as a wholly social construction.

Genetic ancestry tests advertise "ethnicity estimates" (Senator Elizabeth Warren appealed to the perceived authority of DNA this week to demonstrate her Native American heritage, in response to mocking by President Trump), and some disease-risk genes have turned out to be more common among certain genetic ancestry groups. Doctors use patients' self-identified race as a proxy for geographic ancestry, because individual readouts of DNA are costly, and though the correlation is imperfect, it exists.

As DNA databases tied to medical records and personal questionnaires have reached a critical mass for individuals of European descent, moreover, so-called polygenic scores that synthesize the hundreds or thousands of genes that contribute to many human traits into a single number are being developed to predict health risks, and in some cases, behavior.

Last summer, researchers developed a score that can roughly predict the level of formal education completed by white Americans by looking at their DNA. And while those scores cannot yet be compared among racial or population groups, the new techniques have prompted some scientists to feel it is the field's responsibility to head off predictable misrepresentations.

"You have to make a judgment when you have powerful information that can be misused," said David Reich, a Harvard geneticist who has publicly called on colleagues in a recent book and in a New York Times Op-Ed to more directly address the prospect of identifying genetic differences between populations in socially sensitive traits.

There is no evidence, scientists stress, that environmental and cultural differences will not turn out to be the primary driver of behavioral differences between population groups.

At the same time, the advances in genetic technology have put white supremacists into a kind of anticipatory lather.

"Science is on our side," crowed Jared Taylor, the founder of the white nationalist group American Renaissance, in a recent video that cites Dr. Reich's book.

Dr. Reich was among those to decline an invitation to lead a discussion on the topic at the San Diego meeting. "I really wanted to return to research," he said.

The widespread uncertainty among Americans over what scientists know about genetic differences between racial groups, experts say, has left many flummoxed in the face of white supremacist claims that invoke genetics.

"I was surfing my favorite dumb picture site and I came across a post trying to prove racism with science," a community college student in Florida wrote to Jun Z. Li, a University of Michigan geneticist whose work has been invoked to buttress racist claims of white intellectual superiority. "I read through the paper myself but I do not have the education or experience to understand and make sure I have a coherent counter argument."

For white Americans half-inclined to blame nonwhite immigrants or African-Americans for perceived social problems, the veneer of a scientific rationale for white superiority, researchers say, can tip them toward racial resentment. It can be more effective than base appeals to tribalism, especially for the educated demographic the far-right has been targeting.

And while much of current white nationalist rhetoric is framed in terms of preserving a white cultural identity, experts say it relies on a familiar narrative of immutable biological differences. On a YouTube talk show earlier this year, for instance, Gavin McInnes, founder of the Proud Boys, whose appearance set off a brawl outside a Republican club in Manhattan last week, echoed the pet white supremacist theory that the environmental challenges of cold winters explain the supposed higher intelligence of northern Europeans.

Some geneticists have penned blog posts explaining why new genetic tools will not support white nationalist claims that average behavioral differences between groups are immutable. Others — including Dr. Li — have replied directly to individual queries.

And when a blogger at the far-right Unz Review noted that the DNA variations associated with high IQ in a 2017 study of Europeans were at the lowest frequency among Africans, the study's lead author, Danielle Posthuma, wrote in a published reply that such cross-population comparisons were spurious.

"This," she wrote, "is a very deep-rooted misunderstanding."

Many geneticists at the top of their field say they do not have the ability to communicate to a general audience on such a complicated and fraught topic. Some suggest journalists might take up the task. Several declined to speak on the record for this article.

And with much still unknown, some scientists worry that rebutting basic misconceptions without being able to provide definitive answers could do more harm than good.

"There are often many layers of uncertainties in our findings," said Anna Di Rienzo, a human genetics professor at the University of Chicago. "Being able to communicate that level of uncertainty to a public that often just sees things in black and white is very, very difficult."

As a step toward changing that, Dr. Di Rienzo has helped organize a meeting of social scientists, geneticists and journalists at Harvard next week to discuss the social implications of the field's newest tools.

Participants have been promised that the meeting will be restricted to some three-dozen invitees and that any remarks made there will be confidential.

And David L. Nelson, a Baylor College of Medicine geneticist who is president of the human genetics society, says it will not stay completely quiet on the issue, promising a statement later this week.

"There is no genetic evidence to support any racist ideology," he said.

AMY HARMON is a national correspondent covering the intersection of science and society. She has won two Pulitzer Prizes, for her series "The DNA Age," and as part of a team for the series "How Race Is Lived in America."

Geneticists Criticize Use of Science by White Nationalists to Justify 'Racial Purity'

BY AMY HARMON | OCT. 19, 2018

IN AN UNUSUAL STATEMENT on the role of science in the resurgence of white supremacy in America, the American Society of Human Genetics on Friday denounced "attempts to link genetics and racial supremacy."

The statement, which appears in the November issue of the group's scientific journal, The American Journal of Human Genetics, said the concept of "racial purity" was scientifically meaningless. The group has about 8,000 members and is the largest professional organization of scientists who study human genetics.

As newly visible and often-virulent groups of white nationalists have invoked genetic research to claim racial superiority, some geneticists have suggested that the field was not doing enough to counter the claims.

Some white nationalists have used research on the ability to digest lactose in milk as adults as a sign of racial identity. And some white nationalist messaging falsely suggests that the existence of genetic markers in people whose ancestors came from different continents mean there are genetic distinctions in behavioral traits like intelligence.

Though science is not much in evidence when white nationalists take to the streets chanting slogans like "You will not replace us," scholars of racist ideology say contemporary white racism draws on the trope of "natural" racial hierarchy used to justify the enslavement of African-Americans, the American eugenics movement in the early 20th century and Nazi "racial hygiene" laws.

The topic has been much discussed on the side at the group's annual meeting this week.

"As human geneticists, we cannot 'just focus on our research,' " one geneticist, Melissa Wilson Sayres of Arizona State University, said

Thursday night on social media. "We cannot pretend that our research isn't being misused. Doing so is being actively complicit with white supremacy/nationalism."

The statement by the genetics association came after an article in The New York Times examined how scientists who study human genetic diversity were struggling to respond to the racist misuse of science, even as their tools to discover how human populations vary genetically become more powerful.

In a widely read Op-Ed in The New York Times earlier this year, the Harvard geneticist David Reich wrote that "arguing that no substantial differences among human populations are possible will only invite the racist misuse of genetics that we wish to avoid."

The genetics group's statement is a step toward trying to equip the public with the tools to understand the evolutionary processes that give rise to patterns of human genetic diversity, geneticists said. It explains that genetic variation between human populations is linked to patterns of migration and the mixing of populations throughout history. Given how much mixing has occurred, it says, the white supremacist notion of racial purity is "scientifically meaningless."

It also explains a distinction between race and ancestry that geneticists say has been muddled by the rise of commercial ancestry tests.

"Although a person's genetics influences their phenotypic characteristics, and self-identified race might be influenced by physical appearance," the statement said, "race itself is a social construct," meaning it has no biological basis. "Black," for instance, is a socially defined term that includes many Americans who have a majority of European ancestry.

The statement encourages human geneticists to begin engaging with the public on questions of race, ancestry and genetics.

"In public dialogue, our research community should be clear about genetic knowledge related to ancestry and genomic diversity," it says. "There can be no genetics-based support of claiming one group as superior to another."

Why the Announcement of a Looming White Minority Makes Demographers Nervous

BY SABRINA TAVERNISE | NOV. 22, 2018

WASHINGTON — The graphic was splashy by the Census Bureau's standards and it showed an unmistakable moment in America's future: the year 2044, when white Americans were projected to fall below half the population and lose their majority status.

The presentation of the data disturbed Kenneth Prewitt, a former Census Bureau director, who saw it while looking through a government report. The graphic made demographic change look like a zero-sum game that white Americans were losing, he thought, and could provoke a political backlash.

So after the report's release three years ago, he organized a meeting with Katherine Wallman, at the time the chief statistician for the United States.

"I said 'I'm really worried about this,' " said Dr. Prewitt, now a professor of public affairs at Columbia University. He added, "Statistics are powerful. They are a description of who we are as a country. If you say majority-minority, that becomes a huge fact in the national discourse."

In a nation preoccupied by race, the moment when white Americans will make up less than half the country's population has become an object of fascination.

For white nationalists, it signifies a kind of doomsday clock counting down to the end of racial and cultural dominance. For progressives who seek an end to Republican power, the year points to inevitable political triumph, when they imagine voters of color will rise up and hand victories to the Democratic Party.

But many academics have grown increasingly uneasy with the public fixation. They point to recent research demonstrating the data's power to shape perceptions. Some are questioning the assumptions the Census Bureau is making about race, and whether projecting the American population even makes sense at a time of rapid demographic change when the categories themselves seem to be shifting.

Jennifer Richeson, a social psychologist at Yale University, spotted the risk immediately. As an analyst of group behavior, she knew that group size was a marker of dominance and that a group getting smaller could feel threatened. At first she thought the topic of a declining white majority was too obvious to study.

But she did, together with a colleague, Maureen Craig, a social psychologist at New York University, and they have been talking about the results ever since. Their findings, first published in 2014, showed that white Americans who were randomly assigned to read about the racial shift were more likely to report negative feelings toward racial minorities than those who were not. They were also more likely to support restrictive immigration policies and to say that whites would likely lose status and face discrimination in the future.

Mary Waters, a sociologist at Harvard University, remembered being stunned when she saw the research.

"It was like, 'Oh wow, these nerdy projections are scaring the hell out of people,' " she said.

Beyond concerns about the data's repercussions, some researchers are also questioning whether the Census Bureau's projections provide a true picture. At issue, they say, is whom the government counts as white.

In the Census Bureau's projections, people of mixed race or ethnicity have been counted mostly as minority, demographers say. This has had the effect of understating the size of the white population, they say, because many Americans with one white parent may identify as white or partly white. On their census forms, Americans can choose more than one race and whether they are of Hispanic origin.

Among Asians and Hispanics, more than a quarter marry outside their race, according to the Pew Research Center. For American-born Asians, the share is nearly double that. It means that mixed-race people may be a small group now — around 7 percent of the population, according to Pew — but will steadily grow. Are those children white? Are they minority? Are they both? What about the grandchildren?

"The question really for us as a society is there are all these people who look white, act white, marry white and live white, so what does white even mean anymore?" Dr. Waters said. "We are in a really interesting time, an indeterminate time, when we are not policing the boundary very strongly."

The Census Bureau has long produced projections of the American population, but they were rarely the topic of talk shows or newspaper headlines.

Then, in August 2008 at the height of Barack Obama's campaign for president, the bureau projected that non-Hispanic whites would drop below half the population by 2042, far earlier than expected. (The projections, which change with birth, death and migration rates, have also placed the shift in 2050 and in 2044.)

"That's what really lit the fuse," said Dowell Myers, a demographer at the University of Southern California, referring to the 2008 projection. "People went crazy."

It was not just white nationalists worried about losing racial dominance. Dr. Myers watched as progressives, envisioning political power, became enamored with the idea of a coming white minority. He said it was hard to interest them in his work on ways to make the change seem less threatening to fearful white Americans — for instance by emphasizing the good that could come from immigration.

"It was conquest, our day has come," he said of their reaction. "They wanted to overpower them with numbers. It was demographic destiny."

Dr. Myers and a colleague later found that presenting the data differently could produce a much less anxious reaction. In work published this spring, they found that the negative effects that came from reading about a white decline were largely erased when the same people read about how the white category was in fact getting bigger by absorbing multiracial young people through intermarriage.

It is unclear exactly when the idea of a majority-minority crossover first appeared, but several experts said it may have surfaced in connection with the 1965 Voting Rights Act.

Ms. Wallman, the chief statistician for the United States from 1992 to 2017, who helped develop the first governmentwide standard for data on race and ethnicity that came into use in the late 1970s, said she did not like having to categorize by race, but that the government had to for oversight.

"I wish we didn't have to ask," she said. "But to me, that's the rock and the hard place."

Race is difficult to count because, unlike income or employment, it is a social category that shifts with changes in culture, immigration and ideas about genetics. So who counts as white has changed over time. In the 1910s and 1920s, the last time immigrants were such a large share of the American population, there were furious arguments over how to categorize newcomers from Europe.

But eventually, the immigrants from eastern and southern Europe came to be considered white.

That is because race is about power, not biology, said Charles King, a political science professor at Georgetown University.

"The closer you get to social power, the closer you get to whiteness," said Dr. King, author of a coming book on Franz Boas, the early 20th-century anthropologist who argued against theories of racial difference. The one group that was never allowed to cross the line into whiteness was African-Americans, he said — the long-term legacy of slavery.

To Richard Alba, a sociologist at the City University of New York, the Census Bureau's projections seemed stuck in an outdated classification system. The bureau assigns a nonwhite label to most people who are reported as having both white and minority ancestry, he said. He likened this to the one-drop rule, a 19th-century system of racial classification in which having even one African ancestor meant you were black.

"The census data is distorting the on-the-ground realities of ethnicity and race," Dr. Alba said. "There might never be a majority-minority society; it's unclear."

Asked for a response to Dr. Alba's critique, a Census Bureau spokesman said in an email that "we constantly consult with stakeholders, and scholars, including Richard Alba and other federal agencies to improve our techniques, methodologies, and testing of population projections."

William Frey, a demographer at the Brookings Institution, argued that the Census Bureau was doing the best that it could at a time when society was changing quickly. He was skeptical that today's Asians and Hispanics were analogous to the white ethnic Americans of the 20th century, and believed that a less conservative count would not do much to change the bigger picture. Besides, it is not the job of academics to protect people from demographic change, he said.

"Irrespective of the year, or the turning point, the message needs to come out about what the actual facts are," Mr. Frey said. "We are becoming a much more racially diverse society among our young generation."

Others say they are not sugarcoating statistics, but showing that the numbers have many interpretations, and that white-versus-everyone-else is only one. It not only reduces the American patchwork to a crude, divisive political formula, they say, but perhaps more important — with the categories in flux — it might not even be true.

The Census Bureau released new projections this year in March filled with data about the country's future. In the coming decades, adults 65 and older will outnumber children for the first time in the country's history. The share of mixed-race children is set to double.

But there was no mention of a year when white Americans would fall below half the population.

When asked about the change, a spokesman for the Bureau said: "It was just us getting back to sticking to data."

CHAPTER 2

The Tools of White Nationalism

White nationalists have become increasingly public in recent years. As domestic terrorism has been linked to white nationalist beliefs, journalists have begun to examine how white nationalists have organized themselves. The Internet provides a safe haven for people to share their beliefs, and groups, organized by individuals such as Richard Spencer, have expanded their outreach to campuses across the country. The articles in this chapter examine how the ideas of white nationalism have spread.

After Neo-Nazi Posting, Police in Whitefish, Mont., Step Up Patrols

BY CHRISTINE HAUSER | DEC. 20, 2016

THE POLICE IN Whitefish, Mont., said Tuesday that they have stepped up patrols and are working with the F.B.I. after a neo-Nazi and white supremacist website listed the names and contacts of local Jews, calling on readers to "take action" against them.

Lt. Bridger Kelch of the Police Department in the town in northwestern Montana said that the force was taking the measures after the website, The Daily Stormer, on Friday published phone numbers, work locations, email addresses and photographs of six Flathead County residents. Several of those targeted were from Whitefish where Sherry Spencer, the mother of the white nationalist leader Richard B. Spencer, lives and owns a building that has been the subject of protests.

The matter has been the topic of national news media articles after a local report in The Missoulian drew widespread attention on social media.

Reached by telephone, Lt. Kelch said Tuesday morning that the department was reviewing social media posts and emails directed at the six people, but that none had risen to death threats. He said the department was conducting patrols, but there had been no reported confrontations in person or by telephone. "We have been looking at any communications," he said.

He added that some of the material had been shared with the F.B.I.

Sandra Barker, the spokeswoman for the agency's Salt Lake City office, whose jurisdiction includes Montana, said in an emailed statement on Tuesday: "The F.B.I. is aware of the issue and is reviewing to determine if there is a violation of federal law."

The Daily Stormer article was written by Andrew Anglin, who has been described by the Southern Poverty Law Center as a neo-Nazi. The post was filled with anti-Semitic slurs, and yellow stars reminiscent of the ones Jews were forced to wear by the Nazis were superimposed on photographs of the six: a lawyer, a real estate agent, a boy identified as their child, two rabbis and an activist.

"So Then — Let's Hit Em Up. Are y'all ready for an old fashioned Troll Storm?" he wrote. While he also said he was not advocating "violence or threats of violence or anything even close to that," it was not clear what form of "action" he meant. His past writings have urged readers to scream at Muslims and instill fear in them. In a follow-up on Monday, he wrote that the "lying Jew media" had mischaracterized his original post as advocating violence.

This is the latest stir in Whitefish involving Mr. Spencer, a part-time resident who is the president of the National Policy Institute and leader of the alt-right movement, a racist, far-right fringe group that has promoted a white nationalist ideology and anti-immigrant, anti-Semitic and anti-feminist views.

Mr. Spencer has quoted Nazi propaganda and railed against Jews, including at a conference sponsored by the institute in Washington last month where members exulted in Donald J. Trump's presidential victory with Nazi-era salutes. Mr. Spencer told the audience of more than 200 people that America belonged to white people and said, "Hail Trump" and "Hail victory!" Mr. Trump has disavowed their support.

Mr. Spencer's rise on the national stage has brought scrutiny to Whitefish, which has a population of about 6,000, and is in a popular ski area in a county next to the Canadian border. Mr. Spencer, whom the local Daily Inter Lake described as a recent "part-time resident" of Whitefish, has suggested on Twitter that he would run for the congressional seat of Representative Ryan Zinke if Mr. Zinke is confirmed as Mr. Trump's interior secretary.

The Stormer article was published after Mr. Spencer's mother wrote in a post on Medium last week that she had been receiving "terrible threats" because of her son. Ms. Spencer claimed that a realtor with links to local Jewish organizations had said that there would be protests at the building and that its property value would decline.

The realtor was one of the people subsequently named in Mr. Anglin's article. Repeated efforts to reach those targeted by the article were unsuccessful. One of them, a rabbi, declined to comment through an intermediary.

Some of them were supporters or members of the Montana Human Rights Network and its local affiliate, Love Lives Here. Rachel Carroll-Rivas, a co-director of the rights network, said in a telephone interview they have received threatening messages by telephone, through website forms and on social media accounts.

She quoted one message as saying: "All of you deserve a bullet through your skull. Choke on a shotgun and die. All of you would be of greater worth to society as human fertilizer than citizens."

Ms. Carroll-Rivas denied there had been harassment of the Spencers, but she added that rights activists in the Whitefish area had written online about their opposition to the building and its affiliation with Mr. Spencer.

ABC Fox Montana reported last week that tenants at the building, which houses vacation rentals and commercial space in the downtown area, had said their customers were staying away and had threatened to move out.

Mr. Spencer's parents have tried to distance themselves from their son's views, with Ms. Spencer telling ABC in an email that she did not agree with his "extreme positions."

On Saturday, Mr. Spencer's father joined her in writing an op-ed article in The Daily Inter Lake stating that their son and the National Policy Institute "have never had, do not have and will not in the future have" activities at the downtown building.

"We do not endorse the idea of white nationalism," they wrote.

Attack on Alt-Right Leader Has Internet Asking: Is It O.K. to Punch a Nazi?

BY LIAM STACK | JAN. 21, 2017

IS IT O.K. to punch a Nazi?

That is not a brainteaser or a hypothetical question posed by a magazine on Twitter. It is an actual question bouncing around the internet after an attack on a well-known far-right activist, Richard B. Spencer, in Washington after the inauguration of Donald J. Trump as president on Friday.

Mr. Spencer, who is credited with coining the term alt-right and describes himself as an "identitarian," was punched in the head on Inauguration Day by a person clad in black as he was being interviewed by a journalist. At the time of the attack, Mr. Spencer was explaining the meaning of Pepe the Frog, a cartoon figure adopted as a mascot by the alt-right, a racist, far-right fringe movement that is anti-immigrant, anti-Semitic and anti-feminist. Video of the attack shows Mr. Spencer reeling to one side under the force of the blow and his attacker darting through a crowd after landing the punch.

A bystander who chased the attacker later posted a video on YouTube of his encounter with the man. The assailant can be heard telling a friend that the man filming them is "mad at me because I hit Richard Spencer." (The bystander who made the video does not appear to be a supporter of Mr. Spencer and disparagingly refers to the activist in the clip as "a neo-Nazi.")

Mr. Spencer described the incident in a Periscope video he posted on Twitter on Friday. Shortly after the attack, he said, he was spat on by another person. On Saturday, he said he had a black eye.

Mr. Spencer's video was recorded from what he described as "a

TIM GOESSMAN FOR THE NEW YORK TIMES

Richard B. Spencer, a far-right activist, in Whitefish, Mont., in June.

safe space." He said he thought the attack happened, in part, because he was in the wrong place at the wrong time.

"There was an actual anti-fascist rally going on, and I walked into it," he said. Margarita Mikhaylova, a spokeswoman for the District of Columbia Metropolitan Police Department, said on Friday afternoon that Mr. Spencer had not filed a police report.

Video of the attack quickly inspired a flood of jokes and memes online, some of which set the punch to songs like "Born in the U.S.A." Jon Favreau, a former speechwriter for Barack Obama, was one of many who posted a comment.

There was little substantive debate online about the ethics of punching Mr. Spencer. Twitter is not a place where minds are often changed, and the supporters and opponents of the sucker punch were unmoved by one another's quips.

Opponents of the punch tended to say that violence had no place in political debate. Supporters tended to say the punch was funny, and more than a few compared Mr. Spencer's attacker to famous Nazi punchers from pop culture, like Indiana Jones and Captain America.

One person who disapproved of the attack? A longtime writer for the comic book hero Captain America, Nick Spencer. (He said he was not related to Richard Spencer.)

For the record, Richard Spencer says he is not a Nazi. In an interview on Saturday, he said he was a member of the alt-right, which he calls "identity politics for white Americans and for Europeans around the world."

How is that different from Nazism? Nazism is "a historical term" that "is not going to resonate today," he said.

"German National Socialism is a historic movement of the past," Mr. Spencer said. "It arose at a very particular time and had particular motives and ideas and policies and styles, and those aren't mine."

Mr. Spencer said he was worried about being attacked again.

"I don't think I could go out to an inauguration event without bodyguards or a protest or a conference," he said. "I am more worried about going out to dinner on an average Tuesday because these kind of people are roaming around."

On Periscope, Mr. Spencer also expressed concern about the spread of the footage of the attack online.

"I'm afraid this is going to become the meme to end all memes," he said. "That I'm going to hate watching this."

University of Florida Braces for Richard Spencer

BY ANEMONA HARTOCOLLIS | OCT. 17, 2017

RICHARD B. SPENCER, a prominent white nationalist, is scheduled to speak at the University of Florida on Thursday, prompting an outcry over whether his views are protected speech, dividing the campus and putting law enforcement officials on high alert.

The university denied Mr. Spencer's original request to speak on Sept. 12, citing the violent clashes in August between far-right demonstrators and counterprotesters in Charlottesville, Va., as well as threats on social media of a "blood bath" if the speech were allowed. But the university has since relented.

On Monday, reacting to Mr. Spencer's coming appearance, Gov. Rick Scott declared a state of emergency in Alachua County in North Florida, where the university is. The order helps coordinate law enforcement from various jurisdictions. The governor also activated the National Guard, so it can be called if necessary.

The University of Florida president, Kent Fuchs, posted a YouTube message denouncing Mr. Spencer's "message of hate and racism," and urging students to stay away from his event and deprive Mr. Spencer of the attention he seeks.

Far-right rallies and the counterprotests they engender on the left have become a vexing problem for universities, especially public ones, which are struggling to balance their mission of promoting free speech and the exchange of ideas with their responsibility to keep students safe.

WHO IS RICHARD SPENCER?

Mr. Spencer is the president of the National Policy Institute, which describes itself as "an independent research and educational foundation," and has produced papers on issues like racial differences in intelligence and the crime rate among Hispanic immigrants.

ALEX WROBLEWSKI FOR THE NEW YORK TIMES

Richard Spencer at his office in Alexandria, Va., in August. He is scheduled to speak at the University of Florida on Thursday.

He is credited with coining the term "alternative right," or "alt-right," almost a decade ago. He is the American editor of the website Altright.com.

The Southern Poverty Law Center, which monitors hate groups, has called him "a suit-and-tie version of the white supremacists of old, a kind of professional racist in khakis," though Mr. Spencer has denied that he is a white supremacist.

After the presidential election, he saluted an audience of more than 200 at the National Policy Institute's annual conference in Washington with the cry "Hail Trump, hail our people, hail victory!" In response, a number of his supporters gave the Nazi salute.

In May Mr. Spencer, a University of Virginia graduate, led a torch-bearing group in Charlottesville to a statue of Robert E. Lee, the confederate general, that the city wanted to remove. They chanted, "You will not replace us," and "Blood and soil." That dispute led to a bigger

"Unite the Right" rally in Charlottesville in August, which erupted into street violence, leaving one woman dead when a car driven by a man associated with white supremacist groups plowed into a crowd.

Mr. Spencer appeared again in Charlottesville on Oct. 7 at a small torch-lit rally. He did not return a phone call seeking comment on his visit to the University of Florida.

WHY WILL THE COLLEGE LET HIM SPEAK?

After the university denied Mr. Spencer's original request, a local lawyer, Gary Edinger, threatened to sue on First Amendment grounds. Mr. Edinger, a First Amendment lawyer, said in an interview Tuesday that he had taken the case pro bono. His views do not match Mr. Spencer's, he said, adding that he had voted for Bernie Sanders because he wanted a socialist for president.

The university responded to the lawsuit threat by saying that the ban was not supposed to be permanent, and then negotiated conditions of Mr. Spencer's appearance with Mr. Edinger, said Janine Sikes, a spokeswoman for the university.

"Essentially the university opted to agree on a future date that gave us time to plan for safety and security, and certainly have some say in other factors leading to the event, making it during the daytime, for example," Ms. Sikes said. Some colleges ask polarizing speakers to appear during the day to make crowd control easier.

As a public institution, the University of Florida cannot choose speakers based on their point of view, First Amendment experts say.

"The University of Florida can't say we like country music, but we don't like alternative music — or in this case, we like diversity, but we don't like Richard Spencer's message," Clay Calvert, a journalism professor and First Amendment expert at the university, said.

The university is obligated to protect Mr. Spencer from demonstrators exercising what is called "the heckler's veto," Mr. Calvert said. "That's the idea that the First Amendment does not allow an audience of hostile reaction to silence the speaker."

The university said that security was expected to cost $500,000, far more than the $10,500 it is receiving from Mr. Spencer's group to rent space on campus. But the university said it could not legally pass the security costs on to the National Policy Institute.

WHAT ABOUT PROTESTS?

Far-right activists and counterprotesters have clashed in or around other campuses, including the University of California, Berkeley, Evergreen State College in Washington State and the University of Virginia. The counterprotesters have often been led by Antifa, or anti-fascists, wearing black masks and sometimes wielding pepper spray and other weapons.

The Orlando Antifa has alerted followers to Mr. Spencer's appearance at the University of Florida. It reacted to the announcement that the National Guard was being mobilized with a tweet, "Remember the last time the national guard was invited to a university campus? #NoNazisAtUF." The message was accompanied by the famous photo of an anguished woman kneeling over the body of a Kent State University student shot dead by the National Guard during a protest against the Vietnam War in 1970.

A group called No Nazis at UF has formed, consisting of students, community members and others, and about 90 of them marched to the administration building on Monday to protest Mr. Spencer's appearance.

"Peaceful protests are certainly welcome," Ms. Sikes, the university spokeswoman, said. In a provision that may be aimed at Antifa as well as Antifa's opponents, the police are banning torches, masks and anything that can be used as a weapon at the speech.

Mr. Spencer will be appearing at the school's Phillips Center for the Performing Arts. A security checkpoint will be set up, and 700 tickets will be handed out there on a first-come, first-serve basis, according to altright.com, raising the possibility that many of those attending will be there to heckle him.

WHAT ARE OTHER UNIVERSITIES DOING?

Mr. Spencer's requests to speak have been rejected by Pennsylvania State University, Michigan State, Louisiana State and the University of North Carolina at Chapel Hill. Soon after the Charlottesville violence, Texas A&M canceled his planned Sept. 11 appearance there. But the University of Cincinnati last week said that it would grant Mr. Spencer a venue, with the date to be determined.

A lawsuit was filed on Mr. Spencer's behalf against Michigan State. A similar lawsuit, against Auburn University, resulted in a federal judge's ruling that he be allowed to speak there this past spring.

Some universities have rules requiring that speakers be invited by a student or student group. But the University of Florida has no such requirement.

Although universities are now dealing with protests and violence surrounding speakers on the right, there have been other eras when speakers on the left were the target.

There were protests against the University of Florida for allowing Abbie Hoffman, the Yippie leader and member of the Chicago Seven, to appear in 1970, Mr. Calvert said, and for letting a lieutenant of Louis Farrakhan, leader of the Nation of Islam, speak in the 1990s.

"It kind of shows the viewpoint neutrality of the First Amendment," Mr. Calvert said. "You've got to take them all."

ALAIN DELAQUÉRIÈRE contributed research.

White Nationalist Richard Spencer Is Barred From Speaking at a Federal Building

BY NOAH WEILAND | NOV. 2, 2017

WASHINGTON — An anti-immigrant group led by the white nationalist Richard B. Spencer was told on Thursday that it could not hold its annual conference in a federal office building, just blocks from the White House, because of security concerns raised by the building's management company.

The decision prompted new questions over when, and how, nativist groups are allowed to speak in public spaces.

Mr. Spencer is the president of the National Policy Institute, which promotes itself as a "research and educational foundation." It had planned to hold its meeting on Nov. 19 at the Ronald Reagan Building and International Trade Center in downtown Washington, where the conference took place last year.

Mr. Spencer, who lives in the Washington area, did not respond to a request for comment on Thursday. He told The Washington Post that he was "shocked" when he learned that the building turned down his request to use its space, saying that it seemed "to be a First Amendment issue."

It is not the first time Mr. Spencer's group has asked to hold an event on public property — or, at least, in places that receive federal funds — and been turned away. But it underscores the simmering debate over giving ground for Mr. Spencer and his following to gather.

Michigan State University, Ohio State University and Pennsylvania State University have all recently denied Mr. Spencer the space to speak on campus. But he was permitted to book a speaking venue last month at the University of Florida — though it led to a campuswide outcry and a state of emergency declaration by Rick Scott, the Florida governor.

The right to reserve event space at the Reagan building comes with its own idiosyncrasies.

Owned by the General Services Administration, it is the first and only federal building dedicated to government and private use. The Reagan building is operated by Trade Center Management Associates, a private firm that oversees event spaces in the sprawling complex.

Debra Cope, a spokeswoman for the management group, said the Reagan building "is unique in that it is a public-private partnership that operates differently from other federal buildings."

In a statement, a General Services Administration spokeswoman said that the agency does not have the authority to consider requests to hold events in the part of the building that Mr. Spencer sought to reserve.

The building management's misgivings are partly a response to last year's conference, which drew hundreds of protesters and required dozens of police officers to control the crowd. Ms. Cope described "violent incidents," arrests and threats to building employees during that protest, and noted that the building was damaged in some places. Additionally, she said, Mr. Spencer's meeting and the protests against it disrupted another event in the building that was taking place at the same time.

Last year's commotion did not deter Mr. Spencer's plans to return to the site for this year's annual meeting. In August, he urged supporters to "join us in Washington" in an email promoting the conference at the Reagan building.

That same month, Mr. Spencer was a keynote speaker at a white nationalist march in Charlottesville, Va., to protest the removal of a statue of Robert E. Lee in a city park. A 32-year-old woman, Heather D. Heyer, was killed when one of the protesters plowed his car into a crowd of people who were holding a counterdemonstration against the white nationalists.

The Reagan building management said in a statement that it rejected Mr. Spencer's application in part because of the National Policy Institute's participation in the Charlottesville protests.

Mr. Spencer may have a valid complaint about being barred from speaking in a space owned by the government, said Laura Beth Nielsen, a professor at Northwestern University and a research professor at the American Bar Foundation. But, she said, "that does not mean he has a winning case."

"One thing most people don't know: The First Amendment only prohibits the government from restricting your speech," said Ms. Nielsen, who specializes in matters of hate speech and First Amendment rights. "The question is, 'How do you think about the kind of speech that might pose a threat of violence? Whose obligation is it to secure the space?' "

"The government can restrict speech when they think the person is going to incite lawless activity," she added. "It's not just that it can. It might be obligated to."

Thursday's decision could hint at a more theatrical standoff between Mr. Spencer and the federal government in the future — especially if taxpayers have to pay the bill for the police and other security forces to keep his events under control.

"Of course the state can't stop that person from speaking," Ms. Nielsen said. "But what's our financial and moral obligation to give that speech a platform when it would be really expensive to do that safely?"

The Far Right Has a New Digital Safe Space

ANALYSIS | BY AMANDA HESS | NOV. 30, 2016

WHEN THE WHITE nationalist leader Richard B. Spencer was suspended from Twitter recently, he hopped over to YouTube to address his supporters. "Digitally speaking," he said, Twitter had sent "execution squads across the alt-right." He accused Twitter of "purging people on the basis of their views," calling it "corporate Stalinism." Then he mapped out a path forward. "There's obviously Gab, which is an interesting medium," he said. "I think that will be the place where we go next."

Gab is a new social network built like a hybrid of Twitter and Reddit — posts are capped at 300 characters, and the crowd votes to boost or demote posts in the feed. But Gab's defining feature is its user guidelines, or rather, its lack thereof. Gab bans illegal activities — child pornography, threats of violence, terrorism — and not much else. "Facebook, Twitter and Reddit are taking the path of censorship," Utsav Sanduja, Gab's chief communications officer, told me via email. "Gab does not."

Think of Gab as the Make America Great Again of social sites: It's a throwback to the freewheeling norms of the old internet, before Twitter started cracking down on harassment and Reddit cleaned out its darkest corners. And since its debut in August, it has emerged as a digital safe space for the far right, where white nationalists, conspiracy-theorist YouTubers and minivan majority moms can gather without liberal interference.

This election laid bare the ideological divide on social media, and since the election, the rift has deepened. Just as dejected Hillary Clinton supporters have come together in Pantsuit Nation — a "secret" Facebook group of nearly four million members — some on the right have found their postelection online oasis in the invitation-only Gab.

Gab's 25-year-old founder, Andrew Torba, dreamed up the site after reading reports that Facebook employees suppress conservative articles on the site. Mr. Torba — who previously created Kuhcoon, a system for running automated Facebook ad campaigns (it's now called Automate Ads) — is a rare conservative Christian tech C.E.O. Gab is a corrective to what he dubs "Big Social," and it's based on what the company calls "a pluralistic ethos of mutual respect and toleration of dissonant views."

When other social sites push out disruptive users, Gab opens its arms. Recently, Twitter beefed up abuse rules to police not only threats but also hate speech "against a race, religion, gender, or orientation." (The move presaged the purge that swept up Mr. Spencer.) And Reddit erased a community called Pizzagate, where conspiracy theorists had gathered to spin lies about Democratic pedophiles operating out of a D.C. pizzeria. On Gab, the topic is always trending.

All the big-name Twitter castaways have resurfaced here: In addition to Mr. Spencer, there is Milo Yiannopoulos, the Breitbart editor who was barred from Twitter for siccing trolls on the "Ghostbusters" actress Leslie Jones; Pax Dickinson, the former Business Insider chief technology officer who rebranded himself as a victim of P.C. culture when he was sacked for posting sexist tweets; and Tila Tequila, the reality TV star who was booted from Twitter after posting racial slurs and pro-Nazi stuff. Gab has also attracted the cutting conservative commentator Ann Coulter; the right-wing media guerrilla Mike Cernovich; and the disinformation king Alex Jones, founder of Infowars. Gab now hosts 98,000 accounts, with tens of thousands more hopeful members on a wait list.

Right-wing rhetoric pervades the site, even the lifestyle and sports categories. With more than 28,000 followers, Mr. Yiannopoulos is one of the site's biggest stars, though he rarely posts anything. On election night, Mr. Torba excitedly live-Gabbed Donald J. Trump's victory, then wrote, "Gab is going to be absolutely massive under President Trump."

The site has a broader conservative coalition than the largely young, mostly male crews camped out on Reddit's Trump forums or slithering around the anonymous message board 4chan. The Facebook factions have found a home here, too. Recently a woman named Lisa posted to Gab: "Hi folks. I'm a #gabmom from Ohio and this is my 1st post. Still trying to figure the format out but thanks for the site Andrew!" Her note has been up-voted more than 200 times. Gab's mascot is a frog, which Mr. Torba claims is based on religious and natural sources associating frogs with exodus and rebirth. Many users see it as a wink to Pepe the Frog, the internet cartoon that became a 4chan icon and — after being dressed up online in Nazi insignia — was declared a hate symbol by the Anti-Defamation League. But plenty of non-meme-fluent Gab users just see it as a cute mascot, "Gabby."

High on Mr. Trump's win, Gab users are pretty upbeat. Part of the reason that Gab's anti-anti-harassment rules work so well, so far, is that most people agree with one another. And one of those points of agreement is that anti-Semitism is tolerable, if not exactly preferred. On Twitter, anti-Semitic and racist trolls prowl around, pouncing on users while dodging the site's moderators. But on Gab, anti-Jewish rhetoric is slung casually and liberally. One user, angry that his content had just been downvoted, wrote, "Thanks to the #Jew that just stopped by." Andrew Auernheimer, a white supremacist troll known as weev, kicked off a minor censorship debate when Gab erased his bio, which advocated the rape, torture and murder of Jews. When one user advised weev to be more careful to avoid trouble with the law, another accused him of being Jewish.

While mainstream social networks are promising to crack down on "fake news," Gab clears the runway for posts like "Satanic PizzaGate Is Going Viral Worldwide (Elites Are Terrified)" to pick up speed. Ricky Vaughn, a pseudonymous white nationalist (he takes his name from Charlie Sheen's character in "Major League") also barred from Twitter, posted to Gab that Twitter is effectively dead and should now be used only to pull off "skirmishes" against Twitter denizens. Gab would be a convenient base for recruiting more digital foot soldiers to that cause.

Behind the rah-rah free speech attitude, dissenting opinions on Gab are quashed in their own way. Overtly racist accounts were created by enemies to make Gab look bad, Mr. Torba said in a post. "Without a doubt," he wrote, "we have fake shill profiles attempting to play into the media narrative."

But some have worried that the site's insulation can dampen their message. "Now that Twitter is purging everyone, I think it's important for Gab to branch out and attract leftists so we're not just preaching to the choir," wrote Paul Joseph Watson, editor at large at Infowars.

When I asked why the site leans conservative, Mr. Sanduja denied that Gab had any ideological bent. "We challenge this premise completely — to the contrary, Gab has a number of diverse users globally," he wrote. (There is a politely argumentative Democrat who goes by the handle @Democrat, for instance.) But he added that right-wing users would be naturally drawn to Gab. "When a group of people are being systematically dehumanized and labeled as the alphabet soup of phobias," he wrote, "they will look for a place that will allow them to speak freely without censorship and devoid of Social Justice bullying."

But that's the trick, isn't it? You can't sell a social destination where conservatives are free from liberal pestering and expect the pitch to resonate across the spectrum. Even the idea that harassment rules are oppressive — instead of protective of the vulnerable — is itself a pointed worldview. I suspect that any concern about inclusion will be assuaged by the comfort of chatting with people who think and talk the same way. It's the next logical step after all the blocking and muting on Twitter and filtering and unfollowing on Facebook split America into two social media realities. Where there once was a bubble, now there's a wall.

On Gab, an Extremist-Friendly Site, Pittsburgh Shooting Suspect Aired His Hatred in Full

BY KEVIN ROOSE | OCT. 28, 2018

EARLY SATURDAY, MOMENTS before the police say he barged into a Pittsburgh synagogue and opened fire, Robert Bowers's anti-Semitic rage finally boiled over as he posted one last message online.

But he did not turn to Facebook or Twitter. Instead, the man accused of killing 11 people went to Gab, a two-year-old social network that bills itself as a "free speech" alternative to those platforms, and that has become a haven for white nationalists, neo-Nazis and other extremists. There, he posted a signoff to his followers.

The shooting in Pittsburgh came on the heels of another violent episode involving social media extremism. Cesar Sayoc Jr., the suspect in the pipe bomb mailing campaign, had a history of posting hateful and violent messages on Facebook and Twitter that were laced with misinformation and conspiracy theories.

There have long been hateful enclaves online, and chat rooms and message boards where white nationalists, neo-Nazis and other extremists have congregated. But the popularity of mainstream mega-platforms like Twitter, Facebook and YouTube has created environments in which misinformation and hate can multiply, and where extremists can attempt to convert — or "red pill," in the parlance of right-wing internet activists — a new generation to their cause.

Social media platforms like Facebook and Twitter, once guided by the principle of free speech, have come to realize that an anything-goes approach is ripe for exploitation, and ultimately bad for business.

"The challenge faced by any platform that allows everything permitted under U.S. law is that if left unabated, the most objectionable content will inevitably take over," said Micah Schaffer, a former policy leader at YouTube and Snap who is now a technology policy consultant. "If an online community is dominated by porn, beheadings or white supremacists, most people aren't going to think it's a good place for their baby photos."

Facebook and Twitter's attempts to crack down on hateful and violent speech have been inconsistent, and many objectionable posts still slip through the cracks. (Mr. Sayoc, for instance, was reported to Twitter for making a violent threat against a Democratic television commentator this month, but the company declined to take action against him, a decision it has since said was in error.)

But the companies have made earnest efforts to clean up their platforms — and in the process, they have pushed some extremists to alternative venues like Gab.

Mr. Bowers's affiliation with Gab has already cost the company dearly. On Saturday, the company's web hosting provider, Joyent, said it would stop hosting the site, according to an email posted by Gab on Twitter. Gab's website went offline Sunday night and was replaced with a statement saying that its service would be temporarily inaccessible while it switched to a new hosting provider.

"We have been systematically no-platformed by App Stores, multiple hosting providers and several payment processors," the statement read.

In addition, GoDaddy, the domain name provider, told Gab it had 24 hours to move its domain name to another service, after finding content on the site that promoted violence.

The payment processing platform Stripe, which Gab has used to receive fees for its paid Gab Pro membership level, and which froze Gab's account this month for violating its terms of service, said it was suspending transfers to the company's bank account pending an investigation, according to another email posted to Twitter by Gab. PayPal, another payment processor, canceled Gab's account, saying it had been closely monitoring the site even before Saturday's massacre.

"When a site is allowing the perpetuation of hate, violence or discriminatory intolerance, we take immediate and decisive action," a

PayPal spokesman said. Joyent did not respond to a request for comment. A Stripe spokesman said the company could not comment on individual users for privacy reasons.

Gab, which was started in 2016 by a conservative programmer, Andrew Torba, who was fed up with what he saw as Silicon Valley's left-wing censorship, was a controversial project from the start. The announcement of its introduction doubled as a broadside against political correctness, which the company said had "become a cancer on discourse and culture." Gab, its creator said, would be a social network where all speech would be welcome, no matter how noxious or offensive.

In an email interview on Saturday, Mr. Torba, Gab's chief executive, said that he had not reviewed all of Mr. Bowers's posts, but that the company had turned over information about his account to law enforcement agencies and was cooperating with the investigation.

"Because he was on Gab, law enforcement now have definitive evidence for a motive," Mr. Torba wrote. "They would not have had this evidence without Gab. We are proud to work with and support law enforcement in order to bring justice to this alleged terrorist."

Technically, there was nothing special about Gab at the start — its interface was buggy and unattractive, and it lacked the features of more established social networks. But the platform's intentionally slim rule book attracted a crowd of extremists, including white nationalists and neo-Nazis, who had been banned from other social platforms. Milo Yiannopoulos, the former Breitbart writer whose harassment campaigns got him kicked off Twitter, signed up for an account. So did Andrew Anglin, the founder of the neo-Nazi publication Daily Stormer, and Richard Spencer, the well-known white nationalist.

Within months, Gab had become a last refuge for internet scoundrels — a place where those with views considered too toxic for the mainstream could congregate and converse freely. The site's guidelines prohibit threats of violence, but not hateful speech.

Gab's reputation for accommodating extremism may have been what drew Mr. Bowers to the site. In January, he signed up for an account, and began sharing anti-Jewish images, conspiracy theories about Jews controlling the world, and criticism of President Trump — whom, he implied, was too accommodating of Jewish influence. He appeared to have other social media accounts, but Gab was where he aired his hatred in full. His bio on the site read, "Jews are the children of Satan," and a photo on his profile included the number 1488, a reference to Nazism that is popular among white supremacists.

After Mr. Bowers was named as a suspect in the mass shooting, Gab released a statement saying it "unequivocally disavows and condemns all acts of terrorism and violence." The company spent much of Saturday replying to its critics on Twitter, and deflecting blame by pointing out that Mr. Bowers also had accounts on other social networks. The company boasted that its website was getting a million views per hour in the aftermath of the Pittsburgh shooting.

This is not Gab's first run-in with controversy. Last year, Google banned the company's app for failing to moderate hateful content. (The app was rejected by Apple.) In August, Microsoft threatened to cut off Gab's access to its Azure cloud service after posts surfaced on the site advocating genocidal violence against Jews. The posts were ultimately taken down.

Mr. Torba insisted in his email that the shooting had not changed his mind about Gab's core mission of promoting free speech.

"Twitter and other platforms police 'hate speech' as long as it isn't against President Trump, white people, Christians, or minorities who have walked away from the Democratic Party," he wrote. "This double standard does not exist on Gab."

What did exist on Gab was a flurry of posts made by people who appeared to share Mr. Bowers's hatred for Jews.

The site, which functions like a combination of Twitter and Reddit and claims to have more than 700,000 members, is not exclusively for bigots. It has areas for various interest groups, including cryptocurrency traders, doomsday preppers and fans of Japanese-style animated pornography. But Gab's most popular posts espouse far-right ideology.

"Gab became their safe haven because it was actively recruiting the worst of the worst," said Joan Donovan, a media manipulation researcher with the nonprofit organization Data and Society. "Gab's users have complained of a global Jewish conspiracy to control the internet, where Gab is the only place online where they can network with one another."

In the past several years, as Twitter and Facebook have stepped up their enforcement of policies to prevent hate speech and abuse, some white nationalists and neo-Nazis have been forced to find other ways to communicate.

Discord, a chat app built for video gamers, became a haven of white nationalists last year, who used the service to plan and execute the "Unite the Right" rally in Charlottesville, Va. The company subsequently shut down several large far-right groups, but many have since reappeared.

On Saturday, a Discord channel populated by neo-Nazis filled with chatter and gossip about Mr. Bowers's possible involvement in a mass shooting of Jews. Several members praised Mr. Bowers, while others criticized him for jeopardizing the neo-Nazi movement's long-term prospects by resorting to violence.

"This guy just blew out the kneecaps of the movement in order to kill some no name Jews," one member wrote.

A Discord spokeswoman said the company had investigated and found some accounts that violated its terms of service, which it deleted, although she said the accounts were not directly linked to the shooting.

On Gab, however, the talk was less about Mr. Bowers and the anti-Jewish movement, and more about what was happening to the platform itself. On Saturday, as Gab's service providers began to cut ties, one of the most popular posts on the site speculated that the company was being unfairly targeted because "Gab is the free speech platform Jews want to destroy."

Asked if Gab would be changing any of its policies in response to the mass shooting, Mr. Torba gave an unequivocal answer.

"Absolutely not."

White Supremacists Are Increasingly Using Public Banners

BY MAGGIE ASTOR | MARCH 15, 2018

WHITE SUPREMACISTS ARE increasingly hanging banners in public places, such as from highway overpasses and rooftops, to promote their views, according to a report released on Thursday by the Anti-Defamation League.

"While white supremacists have been using banners for some time, the number of banners deployed in the past 10 months marks an unprecedented trend," the report said. The tactic, it added, is significant because it "can garner widespread attention with very little actual effort involved."

From May 20, 2017, through this Monday, the A.D.L.'s Center on Extremism found, there were 72 such episodes. Before that period, the A.D.L. had not documented any white supremacist banners since Dec. 11, 2016, said Jake Hyman, a spokesman for the group.

Most of those documented in Thursday's report were racist or anti-immigrant in nature, with messages ranging from "America first: End immigration" to " 'Diversity' is a code word for white genocide." Others were anti-Muslim (a banner displayed on an overpass near Dearborn, Mich., home to one of the largest mosques in North America, read "DANGER: Sharia city ahead"), anti-Semitic ("UNjew HUMANITY") or misogynistic ("Feminists deserve the rope").

More than 70 percent were hung by organizations associated with the so-called alt-right, according to the report. One group alone, Identity Evropa, was responsible for around 40 percent: 28 banners in 13 states. Altogether, banners were documented in 21 states.

Identity Evropa describes itself as "a fraternal organization for people of European heritage located in the United States that participates in community building and civic engagement," but the A.D.L. and the Southern Poverty Law Center describe it as a white nationalist group. The A.D.L. wrote in its report that the phrases on Identity Evropa's banners — "Import the third world, become the third world," for example, and "You will not replace us" — were "a sanitized version of the group's true aim, the preservation of 'white American identity' and the promulgation of the idea that America was founded by white people for white people, and was not intended to be a multiracial or multicultural society."

Other organizations have used more explicit language. The Patriot Front, a neo-Nazi group that was behind 30 percent of the episodes the A.D.L. documented, has hung banners that say "For race and nation" and "Americans are white. The rest must go." The group's manifesto declares, "An African may have lived, worked, and even been classed as a citizen in America for centuries, yet he is not American."

Two other neo-Nazi groups, Vanguard America and Atomwaffen, hung smaller numbers of banners. Jimmy Marr, an Oregonian who once drove a truck emblazoned with swastikas, was behind many of the anti-Semitic banners the A.D.L. documented.

More banners were hung in Oregon than in any other state, most likely because of Mr. Marr, the report said. California, Texas and Georgia, where Identity Evropa and the Patriot Front have active chapters, were also heavily affected.

Extremist groups have become more active in the past two years, and have expressed a sense of invigoration since President Trump's election. Hate groups and hate crimes have become more common, and in a report released last month, the A.D.L. found that anti-Semitic episodes had increased 57 percent in 2017 from the year before.

White Supremacists' Use of Campus Propaganda Is Soaring, Report Finds

BY JULIA JACOBS | JUNE 28, 2018

WHITE SUPREMACIST GROUPS are increasingly using propaganda like fliers and posters to spread bigoted messages on college campuses, a new report by the Anti-Defamation League found.

In the past academic year, 292 such incidents were reported — a 77 percent increase from the previous year, according to the report, which was released on Thursday. The stickers, banners and other physical materials included racist and anti-Semitic messages and often targeted Muslims, nonwhite immigrants and L.G.B.T. people.

Spreading propaganda across college campuses has become a popular tactic for white supremacist groups in recent years, said Oren Segal, the director of the A.D.L.'s Center on Extremism.

"They're trying to engage with what they hope are future members of their organizations, followers of their ideology," he said in an interview. "They have put a premium on winning hearts and minds."

As part of this strategy, white supremacist groups try to expand their reach by encouraging anyone with internet access to download the materials and spread their messages, he said.

In recent years, members of the far right — including white supremacists and neo-Nazis — have made themselves increasingly visible at events like a rally in Charlottesville, Va., last year that turned deadly when a man drove a car into a crowd of counterprotesters.

White supremacist groups have also rallied at multiple colleges in the past year in conjunction with speakers like the white nationalist Richard Spencer, events that often intentionally drum up outrage and prompt protests that draw national attention.

Since September 2016, the Anti-Defamation League has recorded 478 instances of white supremacist propaganda at colleges and universities, according to the report. Texas and California were the most frequently targeted states, which the league attributes to more concentrated membership in those states from the most active white supremacist groups.

The anti-immigrant group Identity Evropa was behind nearly half of the 478 reports recorded by the A.D.L. Identity Evropa describes itself as "a fraternal organization for people of European heritage located in the United States that participates in community building and civic engagement," but the A.D.L. classifies it as a white supremacist group and the Southern Poverty Law Center describes it as a white nationalist group.

Far-right groups have increased their activity since President Trump's election, and white nationalist leaders have been encouraged by how the president has spoken about their behavior. In a report released earlier this year, the Anti-Defamation League found that anti-Semitic episodes had increased 57 percent in 2017 from the year before.

The new report documented racist fliers covering photos of black historical figures outside the University of South Carolina's African-American studies program, as well as fliers at multiple schools encouraging students to report undocumented immigrants to Immigration and Customs Enforcement.

Mr. Segal said the Anti-Defamation League provides guidance for universities on how to respond to racist or anti-Semitic propaganda on their campuses, a delicate task that can get complicated when the messaging on the posters is not illegal or even contrary to the school's code of conduct.

At Texas A&M University, Corpus Christi, the administration drew criticism this year from students for its initial response to anti-immigrant fliers posted around campus. Kelly Quintanilla, the university's president, said in a statement to the campus community that such incidents were the "price we pay for our precious right to freedom of speech," prompting demands from student activists for the university to investigate and find who was responsible.

"We felt it was a threat to our immigrant students," said Daniel Yzaguirre, a student activist who recently graduated from the university.

The administration decided to turn the case over to the local district attorney's office, which determined that the fliers were not a threat, according to an email sent to students and staff members.

A spokeswoman for the university could not be reached for comment. Dr. Quintanilla said in a statement to students and employees that she recognized there were a variety of opinions on how administrators should respond to these "vile, yet protected messages."

"Personally, I choose not to be drawn into this divisiveness, because to do so gives the groups who spread hate exactly what they want," she said.

Farther north, administrators at Texas A&M's campus in College Station this year changed the university's policy to heavily restrict the placement of fliers and posters carrying any message — whether it is filled with hate toward a group of people or simply advertising a new club.

"You cannot discriminate by content because of freedom of speech, and so we're careful not to do that," said Amy B. Smith, a university spokeswoman. "We're not going to have fliers of any kind littering our campus."

The hundreds of incidents referred to in the report cover 47 states and the District of Columbia.

In creating its report, the Anti-Defamation League relied mostly on complaints, news reports and posts from the extremist groups themselves, which often publicize these activities, Mr. Segal said. The A.D.L. also aimed to establish the credibility of the reports through photos and confirmation from third parties.

Some Readers Say 'White Nationalist' Normalizes the Charlottesville Protesters

BY THE NEW YORK TIMES | AUG. 14, 2017

The Reader Center is a newsroom initiative that is helping The Times build deeper ties with our audience. We have asked Philip B. Corbett, our standards editor, to discuss the terms we have been using in our coverage of the weekend protests and deadly violence in Charlottesville, Va.

A HANDFUL OF READERS raised concerns over how we described the protesters rallying around a statue of Robert E. Lee in Charlottesville this weekend. Some have questioned whether the term "white nationalist" adequately describes these extremists, suggesting that it comes off as a euphemism. Some readers have said we should use the term "white supremacist" instead.

A reader named Peter Davis emailed us:

> *"I am writing to express my frustration and disagreement with your repeated use of the term 'white nationalist.' I truly believe that using this term is a large part of a huge problem in this country. By using it, you are normalizing these people. These people are 'racists.' They are 'neo-Nazis.'*
>
> *"You are softening the harsh reality of their evil by giving them such a legitimized political title like that.*
>
> *"I strongly urge that you stop using the term. While most of your readers are likely coming from the liberal left, it is still extremely dangerous to slowly normalize and legitimize these racist troublemakers. God forbid you use the term terrorist, which is what they are dabbling in anyway."*

The Times does not have any formal style rules or official definitions for these various terms, but in our coverage of Charlottesville we used a range of descriptions for the groups at the center of the violence, including neo-Nazis, white supremacists, white nationalists and the newest addition to the lexicon, alt-right.

EDU BAYER FOR THE NEW YORK TIMES

A torch-lit parade of neo-Nazis and segregationists marched through the University of Virginia campus in Charlottesville, Va., on Friday night.

The term "white nationalist" seems quite clear in what it stands for: someone who embraces the notion that the United States should be primarily or solely a white society. But any of these terms could apply to those who were marching in the streets, chanting racist and anti-Semitic slogans and displaying the symbols of Nazi Germany and the secessionist South.

As always, our reporters were most intent on describing the actions, the signs and the regalia to make it clear to our readers who the protesters were and what they represent. Those details are probably more revealing than any single label. But there was certainly no effort to soft-pedal or euphemize their views.

NPR Is Criticized After White Nationalist Ranks the Races by Intelligence on Air

BY DANIEL VICTOR | AUG. 10, 2018

AN NPR INTERVIEW with the organizer of last year's white supremacist rally in Charlottesville, Va., ignited complaints on Friday about how news organizations cover white nationalism.

In a "Morning Edition" segment, the radio host Noel King interviewed Jason Kessler, a white nationalist who is planning a rally in Washington this weekend on the anniversary of last year's rally, which was the scene of racist chants and deadly violence.

Ms. King preceded the discussion, which was part of a weeklong series about the anniversary of the Charlottesville rally, with a warning: "Some of what you're about to hear is racist and offensive."

She was correct. In the interview on Friday, which lasted about five minutes, Mr. Kessler relayed junk science and ranked the intelligence of various races.

Ms. King at times pushed back and interrupted Mr. Kessler. Before he made his remarks on race-ranking, which he has supported by citing a political scientist, she said the scholar's work had been "debunked by scientists and sociologists, and is deemed racist by many."

She asked Mr. Kessler: "You said that you're not a white supremacist, but you do think there are differences between races. What are the differences?"

After he answered with his intelligence rankings, claiming black people were the least smart, she said: "You don't sound like someone who wants to unite people when you say something like that. You sound like someone who wants to tick people off."

Critics said the interview allowed Mr. Kessler too much leeway to spread his message.

"The interview appropriately used some degree of skepticism, but not enough," Jonathan Greenblatt, the chief executive of the Anti-Defamation League, said in an interview.

DeRay Mckesson, a prominent voice in the Black Lives Matter movement, was among those who suggested Mr. Kessler never should have been interviewed.

Jason Kessler being given an interview on NPR as if white supremacy is a legitimate policy position is a reminder that many of the (white) people making decisions in the media don't feel impacted by any of this — it's either entertainment or "news" until it hits their doorstep.

— deray (@deray) Aug. 10, 2018

NPR is far from alone among news organizations wrestling with how to cover the rising threat of white nationalism while not inadvertently lending the movement credibility. The New York Times, for one, fielded criticism in November of a profile of a white nationalist, prompting a response from The Times's national editor and the reporter.

Mr. Greenblatt said that simply ignoring the white nationalists and supremacists was not an answer. The A.D.L. has documented an increase in extremist activity in recent years, and he said it was important for news outlets to cover the story so people can understand how bigotry spreads.

But journalists have a responsibility to avoid becoming accidental conduits of hate, he said. Mr. Kessler's views, he added, could have been conveyed without directly interviewing him.

"I don't think it's helpful to hand the microphone to an individual like Kessler, who has demonstrated again and again he's not really interested in contributing to the public conversation," Mr. Greenblatt said.

NPR stood by the report on Friday. Terence Samuel, the deputy managing editor of NPR News, said in an interview that he was "proud of the job Noel did this morning."

"I think it's important for us to cover race and racism, and quite frankly, if you're going to do that, you have to talk to racists," he said. "It's uncomfortable, but we do that all the time."

Kenya Young, the executive producer of "Morning Edition," said editors were satisfied that Ms. King had asked the right questions and pushed back sufficiently. And she disagreed with criticism that Mr. Kessler shouldn't be interviewed.

"I don't know how you tell this story without talking to the person who was at the center of it," she said.

Why Squirrel Hill Is a Target for White Supremacists

OPINION | BY ANDRE PERRY | OCT. 29, 2018

As a black boy growing up in Pittsburgh, I always felt welcome in Squirrel Hill. White nationalists hate the inclusion and diversity that it represents.

"MINEO'S PIZZA HOUSE in Squirrel Hill, Pittsburgh, makes the best pepperoni and sausage pizza in the world."

Those were words to live by as a child growing up in the early 1980s in the black neighborhood of Wilkinsburg, in Pittsburgh's East End. The deliciousness of Mineo's pizza made the five miles my brothers and I biked through the predominately Jewish neighborhood of Squirrel Hill well worth it. But the sweet cheese and fresh meats weren't the only things that brought us back. We didn't dare enter certain neighborhoods for fear of scrapping with white boys or not being served. Squirrel Hill was one of the few nonblack neighborhoods that would welcome a group of black boys.

Up to that point, I hadn't had much experience with people in nonblack communities. But my bike rides to Mineo's taught me there was a difference between the Jews in Squirrel Hill and other white people in Pittsburgh. Later on, I learned what contributed to that difference.

In 1988, I transferred to Peabody High School, in the other significant Jewish neighborhood, Highland Park. It was right next to the majority-black areas of East Liberty and Garfield, and the fully integrated public school reflected the area's diversity. I had history teachers who made connections between the Hebrew Benevolent Congregation Temple bombing in 1958 in Atlanta, and the 16th Street Baptist Church bombing in 1963 in Alabama, solidifying for me how vulnerable black and Jewish communities are to white supremacy.

I learned about Pittsburgh's unique connection to modern Judaism and civil rights. Reform Jewish leaders developed and adopted the Pittsburgh Platform, which states, "We deem it our duty to participate in the great task of modern times, to solve, on the basis of justice and righteousness, the problems presented by the contrasts and evils of the present organization of society."

As an athlete I competed against Jewish boys from another integrated school, Taylor Allderdice in Squirrel Hill. Sometimes after track meets, we got pizza at Mineo's. Squirrel Hill's vibrancy didn't come by chance. We learned how to live together. There was a deliberate investment in inclusion and peace.

The Jewish community has been able to maintain that ethic of inclusion in Squirrel Hill. In 2018, blacks, immigrants and L.G.B.T. people crowd the streets with the same level of comfort I enjoyed as a child. Chatty college students in hoodies sit next to older Jews in skullcaps in coffee shops. When passengers step off the packed city buses along Forbes Avenue, they know they will be able to find whatever they need — an outfit for the weekend, a bite to eat, flowers for a date — in any of the shops on nearby Murray Avenue.

Squirrel Hill is the draw, and the Tree of Life synagogue is its nucleus. The spirit of inclusivity starts there, and spills out in the rest of neighborhood. You see it in the diversity of people and also in the diversity of businesses and cultural events. They are geared to invite and support all the residents of the city — past, present and future.

Squirrel Hill, of course, is not a utopia, and it doesn't represent all of Pittsburgh. There were places in Pittsburgh I could not go to as a child, and where I still would not go as an adult. A fellow Pittsburgh native, Brentin Mock, pointed out in a recent CityLab column, "Squirrel Hill is the change that Pittsburgh wishes to be." The rest of Pittsburgh can learn from Squirrel Hill that diversity is a crucial part of any thriving local economy.

Today the schools in Pittsburgh are less integrated than they were in the 1980s. That means there are fewer opportunities for teachers, or even students, to have meaningful discussions about the violence that is victimizing all of us. On Oct. 25, two black shoppers were killed in a Kroger supermarket, in Louisville, Ky. Two days later, 11 Jews were massacred at the Tree of Life synagogue. If our communities and schools are less integrated, less inclusive, how can teachers or anyone else hope to make the connections for us?

Instead, we have a president whose loose and divisive language sets the table for violence.

My classmates and I may have lived in separate communities, but we learned how to study, play, eat and shop together. We had teachers, schools and synagogues that, in word and deed, made everyone feel welcome and included. Places like Squirrel Hill, Tree of Life and others like them are powerful, but they are not protected. And they will not be as long as President Trump and his followers continue to stoke the white nationalist's greatest fear — inclusion.

ANDRE PERRY is a fellow in the Metropolitan Policy Program at the Brookings Institution.

CHAPTER 3

Profiles of White Nationalists

Who are the leaders of the white nationalist movement? And who are the adherents? In this chapter, journalists investigate the lives and beliefs of the individuals who subscribe to white supremacy, from Dylann Roof, the Charleston shooter, to Christopher Cantwell, whose role in the Charlottesville riots made him a figure of national prominence. In the final article, Richard Fausset embeds himself with a white nationalist in order to find out: What makes someone a white nationalist?

Dylann Roof, Suspect in Charleston Shooting, Flew the Flags of White Power

BY FRANCES ROBLES, JASON HOROWITZ AND SHAILA DEWAN | JUNE 18, 2015

LEXINGTON, S.C. — The Facebook profile picture chosen by Dylann Storm Roof in May is thick with symbolism. It shows Mr. Roof, a scowling young white man, wearing a black jacket adorned with two flags — one from apartheid-era South Africa, the other from white-ruled Rhodesia — that have been adopted as emblems by modern-day white supremacists.

Mr. Roof, 21, was arrested Thursday in North Carolina after law enforcement officers identified him as the suspect in the mass shooting at a black church in Charleston, S.C., on Wednesday night. The shooting left nine dead, including the pastor, the Rev. Clementa C. Pinckney.

Officials said the shooting was being investigated as a hate crime. Although it was not clear if Mr. Roof had actually joined any organized white supremacist groups, people who knew him said that in recent months, a young man they described as extremely shy had begun to harbor racist views and make increasingly violent statements about attacking black people.

Joseph Meek, 20, a childhood friend who reconnected with Mr. Roof this year, said Mr. Roof had changed, spewing racist ideas and talking about wanting "to hurt a whole bunch of people."

"He was saying all this stuff about how the races should be segregated, that whites should be with whites," Mr. Meek said. "I could tell there was something inside him, there was something he wouldn't let go. I was trying to tell him, 'What's wrong?' All he would say was that he was planning to do something crazy."

At first Mr. Meek said he did not take Mr. Roof seriously. But he became worried enough that several weeks ago he took away and hid Mr. Roof's .45-caliber handgun, which Mr. Roof had bought with money given to him by his parents for his 21st birthday. But at the urging of his girlfriend, Mr. Meek returned the weapon because he was on probation and did not want to get into trouble.

Now Mr. Meek and his girlfriend, Lindsey Fry, both of whom are white, say they feel guilt about the shooting. "I feel we could have done something and prevented this whole thing," Ms. Fry said.

Asked why Mr. Roof picked that particular church, Mr. Meek replied, "Because it was a black church."

Another friend, Dalton Tyler, said that Mr. Roof had begun talking about wanting "to start a civil war." But like Mr. Meek, he did not always take Mr. Roof seriously.

Mr. Tyler said on another occasion, the two were driving to a strip club by the zoo when Mr. Roof saw a black woman, used a racist word and said, "I'll shoot your ass."

"I was just like, 'You're stupid,' " Mr. Tyler said. "He was a racist; but I don't judge people."

Mr. Roof has had two previous brushes with the law, both in recent months, according to court records. In February, he attracted attention at the Columbiana Centre, a shopping mall, when, dressed all in black, he asked store employees "out of the ordinary questions" such as how many people were working and what time they would be leaving, according to a police report.

When a police officer questioned Mr. Roof, he "began speaking very nervously and stated that his parents were pressuring him to get a job," but then admitted that he had not asked for applications at any of the stores, the report said.

Asked if he had any contraband, Mr. Roof said no, according to the report, but the officer searched him and found Suboxone, a prescription drug used to treat opiate addiction and frequently sold in illegal street transactions. Mr. Roof admitted that he did not have a prescription for the drug, the report said, and he was arrested and charged with misdemeanor drug possession. The case is pending.

In April, Mr. Roof was charged with trespassing at the same mall. The police report said he had been barred from the mall for a year after the drug arrest. Mr. Roof was convicted on that charge, a misdemeanor.

Mr. Roof's current address is listed in public records as being in this rural speck of a town southeast of Columbia with an overwhelmingly black population. On Mr. Roof's Facebook profile, which was taken down Thursday, many of his 88 friends were black. More than half a dozen cars from the Richland County sheriff's office were parked along the dusty driveway outside the two-story wood-frame home in Eastover. A man in a straw hat came out of the house and told a reporter: "Make your way right back where you came from. Get off the property now."

From school records, Mr. Roof appears to have moved back and forth as a child between Richland County, which includes Columbia and Eastover, and nearby Lexington County to the west. He attended ninth grade twice: at White Knoll High School in Lexington in the 2008-9 school year and, the next school year, at White Knoll until

February 2010, when he transferred to Dreher High School in Columbia. Neither school district had records of his finishing high school.

A neighbor in Eastover, Debra Scott, 50, said that she had seen Mr. Roof walking to and from a nearby market but that she knew very little about him or anyone else who might live in his house. She described the house as "very quiet" and said Mr. Roof "seemed like a normal kid."

But Ms. Scott, who is black, said she was "scared to death" after hearing news reports that Mr. Roof wanted to kill black people. "My concern is that he's saying he's out to kill black people," she said, unaware that he had been arrested. "We're the closest ones to him."

She added that her grandmother had called her Thursday morning and told her: "Get out of that bed. That boy was from Garners Ferry," the name of the street where she and Mr. Roof lived.

Mr. Meek said that as a child, Mr. Roof would sometimes sleep over at his house. He described Mr. Roof as so quiet and shy that "his mom pushed him out of the house and told him to make friends." He added, "Every friend he made, I made for him."

Mr. Roof dropped out of high school after the ninth grade, Mr. Meek said, and the two fell out of touch. But this year, Mr. Roof sent him a Facebook friend request and the two got together again, often to go drinking or to strip clubs. Mr. Roof liked vodka and water, Mr. Meek said, adding, "I never saw him with a girl."

He said Mr. Roof worked in landscaping and seemed to live an itinerant life, sometimes sleeping in his car. In recent weeks his behavior turned more bizarre, as he talked about wanting to burn an American flag and get his neck tattooed with the word "dagger."

The friends last saw Mr. Roof on Tuesday when Ms. Fry found him sleeping in his car parked on a sandy patch in front of Mr. Meek's house. Asked if she considered that odd, Ms. Fry replied, "He does weird things all the time."

FRANCES ROBLES and **JASON HOROWITZ** reported from Lexington, and **SHAILA DEWAN** from New York. **RICHARD A. OPPEL JR.** contributed reporting from New York. **SUSAN BEACHY** contributed research.

Christopher Cantwell, White Nationalist in Vice Video, Braces for Charges

BY MATT STEVENS | AUG. 21, 2017

BY AT LEAST one measure, Christopher Cantwell, a self-described white nationalist, said he believed his decision to be interviewed in a Vice News report had "worked out magnificently."

The documentary has been viewed more than 44 million times since it aired on Aug. 14.

In it, Mr. Cantwell is shown calling for an "ethno-state" and saying that the death of a 32-year-old woman who was killed protesting a white nationalist rally in Charlottesville, Va., on Aug. 12 was justified, adding, "I think that a lot more people are going to die before we're done here."

A week after the broadcast, Mr. Cantwell has emerged as a high-profile activist for the so-called alt-right. In that sense, he said in interviews, it's a victory because he drew the scorn of liberals.

"The first thing you've got to understand is my job is to shock people," Mr. Cantwell, 36, said in the first of two telephone interviews on Friday and Saturday.

But in many other ways, his actions and the public exposure have upended his life.

Since the rally in Charlottesville, the prospect of an arrest has loomed over Mr. Cantwell, who posted a video on Aug. 12 in which he choked back tears.

He gave a phone number that he said the authorities could use to contact him, and he said that since then, his voice mail has been "recording death threats faster than I can listen to them."

Officials at the Commonwealth's Attorney's Office of Albemarle County in Charlottesville said on Monday morning that four warrants had been issued for Mr. Cantwell's arrest. The office referred questions about the nature of the charges to the University of Virginia Police Department. A spokesman at the department did not respond to requests for comment on Friday, Saturday and Monday.

The Boston Globe reported on Thursday that the warrants were related to the "illegal use of gases, and injury by caustic agent or explosive."

In interviews on Friday and Saturday, Mr. Cantwell said that if he were to face such charges, he believed they are connected to an episode he said was photographed by a journalist.

The image, he said, shows "that I'm pepper-spraying a guy straight in his face as he's coming toward me."

"I thought that spraying that guy was the least damaging thing I could do," he added. "In my left hand I had a flashlight. My other option, other than the pepper spray, was to break this guy's teeth. O.K.? And I didn't want to do that. I just wanted him to not hurt me."

In an interview on Monday, Emily Gorcenski, an activist for transgender rights, said she filed a report against Mr. Cantwell with the University of Virginia police on Aug. 12. The night before, she said, she was standing to Mr. Cantwell's right when he used some kind of pepper spray on a group of counter-protesters that demonstrated against the torch-lit march Mr. Cantwell and other white supremacists held on campus.

"He sprayed basically the whole group," Ms. Gorcenski said. "The whole thing was scary. I was targeted by people wearing swastika pins. It was terrifying."

Ms. Gorcenski said she recognized Mr. Cantwell from his YouTube videos, and she had seen him earlier organizing his group at a Walmart parking lot. She said she believed her complaint was the cause of one, but not all, of the charges against him.

Mr. Cantwell, who lives in New Hampshire and hosts a podcast, said he had read The Globe report but had not spoken with the authorities in Virginia. He said he would turn himself in immediately if necessary.

"I don't think I did anything wrong, and I'm looking forward to my day in court," he said on Friday.

On Monday, he said in an email he was contacting his lawyer.

The violence erupted in Charlottesville ostensibly over the planned removal of a statue of a Confederate general there.

The Charlottesville police arrested at least two people in connection with the rally and unrest. The Virginia State Police said it made at least three arrests, and the University of Virginia said its Police Department arrested at least one person at an Aug. 11 demonstration.

Mr. Cantwell rose to prominence days later when Vice News aired its report recapping what happened. The reporter, Elle Reeve, was embedded with white nationalists, and the documentary allowed viewers to see things from their perspectives.

Mr. Cantwell was featured prominently in the report.

In it, he cites Michael Brown, Trayvon Martin and Tamir Rice — whose shooting deaths spurred a nationwide debate about criminal justice and racial profiling — as examples of a black person "behaving like a savage." He also reprimanded President Trump for "giving his daughter to a Jew."

After the rally, he dumped at least four firearms and a knife onto a bed, the video shows. Several times throughout the Vice report, he made it clear that he and other members of the alt-right were capable of violence, saying during the rally that they would kill their opponents "if we have to."

Yet in the video he recorded of himself the day of the rally, Mr. Cantwell said he was "terrified" and "afraid" the police would kill him.

On Saturday, he assailed people he said had inaccurately suggested he was scared about going to prison.

"The problem is that my country has descended to a point where your political opinions get you charged with felonies, and that's what I'm upset about," he said. "I get a little emotional about the fact that all this is going on, and now people want to throw me in prison because I want to save my race and nation."

On Sunday, Mr. Cantwell posted a blog post with what he said might be the final episode of his audio show.

"Tomorrow I'm more than likely going to find myself in a cage facing decades in prison," he wrote. "It is entirely possible that this will be the last time you hear from me."

Reporting was contributed by **JOHN ELIGON**, **FRANCES ROBLES**, **LIAM STACK** and **VIVIAN WANG**. **SUSAN BEACHY** contributed research.

'The Daily' Transcript: Interview With Former White Nationalist Derek Black

BY THE NEW YORK TIMES | AUG. 22, 2017

Derek Black, a former white nationalist and a godson of David Duke, spoke with Michael Barbaro in an episode of "The Daily," a New York Times podcast, that received a particularly intense response on Tuesday. In the podcast, Mr. Black describes his experience growing up in a white nationalist family, taking part in a radio show on his father's website Stormfront.org and how he turned on the white nationalist movement.

This is an unedited transcription from the podcast. Please listen to the corresponding audio before quoting from it.

Derek Black: Yeah, I was born into one of the most prominent white nationalist families in the country.

Michael Barbaro: *Wow.*

D.B.: My godfather for lack of any other word was David Duke, who was married to my mother before I was born ... and then my father started the largest white nationalist website ... Stormfront ... it was the first white nationalist website on the internet, and it has been the largest one ever since. So I grew up with the leadership of the white nationalist movement, all coming over to the house, and when I got older, we'd go to conferences and it was my life.

M.B.: *Derek Black grew up in West Palm Beach, Florida, across from the president's Mar-a-Lago mansion and he used to drive past it almost every day in a red pickup truck with a confederate flag sticker on the back window. His father is Don Black, once a grand wizard of the K.K.K. It sounds like what you're describing is like you're the First Child of American white nationalism?*

D.B.: [Laughs.] Yeah … I knew everybody, I knew everybody who was involved in it, and I knew all the different organizations, and I expected that it would be my life's work to try to advance this. I thought it was the right thing. …

M.B.: *How did you process these ideas of your godfather and your father and your mother and this entire movement as a child, what is white nationalism through the eyes of a child?*

D.B.: It's a really tight knit movement of people. It's important to understand the context that in my family pioneering white nationalism on the web was my dad's goal. That was what drove him from early '90s from beginning of the web, and so growing up … we had the latest computers, first people in the neighborhood to have broadband because we had to keep Stormfront running, and so technology and connecting people on the website, long before social media and the way the web is set up now was his driving purpose, so we were very connected to everybody in the white nationalist movement to everyone in the world. When I was a little kid, I would get on chat rooms in the evening … and I had friends in Australia who I would talk to at a certain hour … I had friends in Serbia I would talk to at a certain hour.

M.B.: *And what would you be saying to each other?*

D.B.: In the late '90s, I was talking to a white nationalist kid, and he was explaining to me the American invasion of Serbia and how it tied to Jewish control of American military.

M.B.: *Wow … not the conventional understanding of the U.S. military action which was to spare people genocide.*

D.B.: Absolutely, yeah. I started a kid's website on Stormfront on my dad's website and so, from the time I was 12, would constantly get death threats and emails.

M.B.: *So you started your own kind of white nationalist website for children?*

D.B.: Yeah ... when ... I'm not sure what age ... 11 or 12 or something I set up pretty basic little web page on there, and posted some essays that I was writing at the time. In some ways — in a lot of ways — that brings people together, I know it brought my family together, fact that you have media coming over as I went on television and newspapers, which were usually coming over to talk to my dad ... and then we'd get really bad stories about us, but we're all working toward a cause ... so the fact that everybody is so opposed to something we know is so right really brought us together.

M.B.: *At this point in your life, when you're a young man and you saw an African-American or you saw a Jewish person, what was going through your mind? What kind of things were you thinking or saying to yourself?*

D.B.: I think my family made a distinction between individuals and big groups ... that there's many opinions on this among white nationalists, there are people who say, "Oh you can't be friends with anyone who's not white." And my family was generally a bit more cosmopolitan ... although I think they've gotten more extreme in the last couple of years —

M.B.: *I have to pause and tell you the notion of a cosmopolitan white nationalist is a little tricky. But I'm going to go with it.*

D.B.: [Laughs.] When you zoom in on it, and it becomes the whole world that you're viewing ... then all the different factions take on a bigger role. So yeah, I think my family — usually, at least, it was definitely my attitude by the time I got to college that individuals are one thing. You talk to people and everybody can be anything and their race is not going to predict an individual's life or anything about them. It's only when you're talking about millions of people that this becomes a defining aspect of humanity.

In reality it is white supremacy. It's just that they wouldn't see it that way. I never saw it that way. My dad — I genuinely believe, who I know very well — does not believe that he is doing something bad to other people. That does not make it untrue, but a lot of these people don't believe that they're actually hurting other people by their policies.

M.B.: *He instead believes what that he's doing something for himself?*

D.B.: He believes that for white people to exist and live and have a country like America was before 1950, everybody needs to be the same color and be together because, race is a real, genetic thing that predicts all this stuff like intelligence and ability, that race is so real that every race in the world should be separated. Saying this and living as I do now sounds delusional, but it is possible for somebody to believe and think that it makes sense.

M.B.: *Derek, can you take me to 2008 and President Obama's election? I don't know exactly how old you were at that moment but do you remember where you were and what you were doing around that time?*

D.B.: In 2008, I was 19 and at the same time as Obama was heading to winning the presidency I had also submitted my name for this local Republican executive committee election which was county level, and I won that. I got 60 percent of the vote.

After he won, David Duke, my godfather, organized a conference for I think it was the weekend after the election. And I went up there ... and it was pandemonium. I knew people who were sobbing, and saying that now there's never going to be another white president again, and that the country is lost, thinking they had to make contingency plans. The thinking of white nationalist leaders at the time was that Barack Obama has won, but now that he's won, you're going to have a huge white backlash against this. And so it became this meeting to try to figure out how to make the movement bigger while he's president.

I had just won that little Republican position, so I was very encouraged that if we told people all the white nationalist talking points, without necessarily saying that we're white nationalists, that we could win elections. Whether they're little county things like that or maybe even larger ones.

M.B.: *My whole talk was the fact that you could run as Republicans, and say things like we need to shut down immigration, we need to fight affirmative action, we need to end globalism, and you could win these positions, maybe as long as you didn't get outed as a white nationalist and get all the controversy that comes along with it. So the Republican Party which had just lost to Barack Obama, your argument was that it could be the vehicle for the mainstreaming of white nationalism or white supremacy?*

D.B.: Yeah, my thinking at the time was that all this backlash, which we eventually did see of white people against having a black president, would have to go into the Republican Party. Because America is a two party system, and the Republican Party would become the white people's party.

M.B.: *Hmm. Then you went to college, so tell me about that.*

D.B.: In 2010, I moved across the state and started college at this little liberal arts college in Florida, which was about three and a half hours from home and it was the first time that I had lived away from home. Nobody knew who I was and I did not volunteer who I was or anything about my background, I made friends, hung out with people and played my guitar on my balcony in my dorm. It was nice to come back from class and be able to talk about history or philosophy or whatever other subject and be around other people.

M.B.: *Hmm.*

D.B.: I'd get up in the morning, and call into my dad's radio show … and talk about the news … and then go to class and hang out with people who were often strong social justice advocates, and trying to live both of those lives was terrifying because I knew that one day somebody was going to type my name into Google.

There was this one really memorable moment where I was sitting in the cafeteria and talking to some people I knew, and one of them discovered this website Stormfront … which is the site that my dad ran and that I had a kid's page on and I that had run the internet radio on for years — and was still running while I was in school, even though I didn't have as much time for it.

And guy sitting across from me found the Lord of the Rings section and showed everybody, and turned around and said, "Can you believe these people are trying to get Lord of the Rings nerds into white nationalism? Isn't this insane?"

And I had founded that section because when movies came out I got super into it, and I figured you could get people who liked with such a white mythos, a few turned on by white nationalism, and more mundanely just wanted to talk about movies, so I had found that 10 years earlier, guy turned it around and I pretended I had never heard of it.

M.B.: *Huh, you just acted as if you had no role in it.*

D.B.: I was like, "What is that? What is Stormfront?"

M.B.: *And so then of course … inevitably it happens. You're found out. The student forum explodes, and you're shunned on campus for a time. But then you get an invitation, right? Tell me about that.*

D.B.: I had a friend on campus who I had gotten to know during my first semester when nobody knew who I was, he was an observant Jew who had Shabbat dinners pretty regularly whenever he was in town on Friday night and he would invite people of atheists and all sorts of different religions. It was just a nice dinner. And so he actually invited me to one of the Shabbats, and I knew him, and so I brought wine.

M.B.: *Even after learning what he did about you?*

D.B.: Yeah, he did. He had read my posts on Stormfront going back years — even the stuff when I was a teenager — and he doubted that he was going to convince me of anything, he just wanted to let me see a Jewish community thing so that if I was going to keep saying these anti-Semitic things that at least I had seen real Jews.

It was ultimately in private conversations with a person I met at the Shabbat dinners ... we would talk about things. Not only white nationalism, but eventually white nationalism. And I would say, "This is what I believe about I.Q. differences, I have 12 different studies that have been published over the years, here's the journal that's put this stuff together, I believe that this is true, that race predicts I.Q. and that there were I.Q. differences in races." And they would come back with 150 more recent, more well researched studies and explain to me how statistics works and we would go back and forth until I would come to the end of that argument and I'd say, Yes that makes sense, that does not hold together and I'll remove that from my ideological toolbox but everything else is still there. And we did that over a year or two on one thing after another until I got to a point where I didn't believe it anymore.

M.B.: *So as you and this friend are going around and around and your mind is changing about this, what's the definitive moment where you make a decision and do something about it?*

D.B.: It was really this letter over the summer of 2013, and I sent it to the Southern Poverty Law Center ... which is an organization my entire life that had been the enemy. They had come after my mother, they had constantly written articles about my father, they had tried to get his website taken down — they had been one of the biggest opponents of my family for my entire life.

M.B.: *And then you turned to them as somebody who would disseminate this letter you wrote?*

D.B.: I did … I turned to them to publish my letter because I knew that their intelligence report was the most widely read thing in the white nationalist world … more so than any white nationalist publication, this was like the gossip mag that the white nationalist world turned to to find out what everybody else was doing. And by sticking my letter on their website, I knew that every white nationalist would see it and every anti-racist would hear about it. The audience was in a lot of ways my own family. I wanted them to know that I understood what we believed, and I was systematically disbelieving each point. And then I just sent it and they published it and when it came out … my dad called me up in the morning and said, "I think you've been hacked, I think your email was hacked and somebody sent this letter."

M.B.: *Wow, he didn't believe you'd written it.*

D.B.: No, we hadn't talked about my beliefs changing. At first he was incredibly sad. He called me a few days after I had written the letter, it was the first time we talked since he first called to tell me he thought I had been hacked, and it was just this sad moment where he said, "I've thought about it and it's really hurting me. I think it might not have been a good idea to have a son … if this is the pain that's going to come from it."

M.B.: *Whoa. He said that he wondered whether it was a good idea to have had a son because of the shame he felt because you had written the letter and rejected everything he stood for?*

D.B.: And I could understand it … he called again later that day and said

I shouldn't have said that I'm sorry. And then we started talking bit by bit. I made the argument that family and political beliefs should not be the same thing and aren't the same thing. He came back at the time with the case that there is nothing in your life experience that would suggest that our family is not a political family, we believe these things. That is the basis of our family the idea that you could be anti white nationalist and that wouldn't affect your relationship to the family is not going to work. It was how we connected it's what kept us together.

M.B.: *Right. This sounds unbelievably painful.*

D.B.: It was.

M.B.: *When's the last time you spoke with him?*

D.B.: Not since before Charlottesville. Not since all this.

My big revelation when I left this movement and no longer talked to anybody in the movement was that most people don't talk about race very often. And so I came to the conclusion that white nationalism is a fringe movement and everybody is aware that it should be a fringe movement, Barack Obama is the president he'll make sure that it stays, remains a fringe movement and I'll just try to quietly fade away and never talk about this again and the future will be fine.

So to begin with, I think it's very important to understand that from the perspective of white nationalists, it's basically the definition of the movement that you're working against the establishment. And that's what every white nationalist event is — it is very easy for the local politicians to condemn it and you expect them to condemn it and there's nothing else that you would dream might happen. It's something that people are proud of ... that you are working even though everybody says you shouldn't. And so that's the context. And all the usual condemnations came from everybody else.

People in Congress, governors, mayors ... people who just wanted to get in their condemnations because everyone knows it's extremely easy to condemn a white nationalist rally. And then on Saturday it was weird that he didn't, everybody took that as a huge victory there were tweets, people commenting online, that's very new, but Tuesday just took my breath away. I was sitting in a coffee shop and I thought the news from this was done when I read that he had come back and he said there were good people in the white nationalist rally and he salvaged their message.

M.B.: *What do you mean when you say he salvaged their message?*

D.B.: The message they were trying to get out was that tearing down Robert E. Lee's statue is an assault on white culture, so if you think that tearing down Robert E. Lee's statue is the wrong choice, then these are your guys that these are the people who are willing to say it but then amidst all the violence and the chaos I think that got lost. You're not going to follow these people even if you believe that.

And in his message saying that these were good people because they're fighting for something that a lot of people believe in, he salvaged the message that they wanted to spread which is that if you believe this too and maybe you're on the edge about whether this is a fringe movement or not, Donald Trump thinks we're fine. I don't think the whole world reads it that way but within the white nationalist movement and anyone who was thinking maybe this might be a movement for me, suddenly being at that that rally becomes a historical moment. What they wanted to do is blow apart that context. To say that if you think Lee statue should stay up, there's no distinction between what you believe and what a white nationalist believes, and it felt like he was agreeing with them.

M.B.: *What do you think the impact of that is having the president in your words salvage their message and make all right what they were doing there in the broader sense?*

D.B.: I think Tuesday was the most important moment in the history of the modern white nationalist movement.

M.B.: *Wow.*

D.B.: It's impossible to say what will happen in the future, like maybe nothing. But if you were on the fence about whether to get involved in this stuff or not, the president's O.K. is the biggest thing that's ever happened. I don't want to be an alarmist and say this is a movement that's going to take over the world. But it's more precarious now than any point in my life on whether this thing as a movement and as a dangerous ideology grows because we don't seem to be as clear as we once were that we have to keep this suppressed we cannot let this be who we are.

M.B.: *I usually have a set of normal reactions in these interviews ... and my vocabulary kind of fails me a little bit ... so I acknowledge that ...*

D.B.: Sure ... no, I understand, I'm in this weird position these days where I have this background, I understand what people at these events and rallies are thinking, but I also know what I know now my experiences and so I can see on one hand where something is horrifying, and on the other, I'm looking at it and wondering why they organize the event like that, why they were so kind of gauche to have swastika flags flying ... and weren't they worried about the messaging and then I come back and say, what is happening to my country ... I have these two experiences, and I have a lot of trouble reconciling them sometimes. As I try to deal with events this week I wonder how much the fact that being in my family and other people I knew were willing to push to try to get people who were maybe on the fence or maybe thought they were being discriminated against or that their kids couldn't get into college because of affirmative action and try to push them a little bit more and try to get them a little but more angry. However much of an effect that had I can't say I don't know.

M.B.: *It sounds like you've given some thought to your own role in this.*

D.B.: It's something I think about everyday, I think.

M.B.: *Derek, you know this I'm sure, there are still pictures of you online as a child attending various far right white nationalist white supremacist conferences, and you've got a little hat on. And you are in it. I'm guessing you don't go back and look, but what do you think when you look back at those images and that version of yourself?*

D.B.: I'm always very conflicted ... that I've come to terms with myself, I'm not too much filled with deep shame all the time. Because I don't know what else I could do. What I wanted to do what would have been more comfortable what I really wanted to do was just leave, never say anything again, disappear off the face of the earth pretend that I had never lived the life that I lived and didn't know anything about white nationalism and never be heard from again... and it was a few more tough conversations that convinced me that wasn't enough because I'd actually done harm ... I tried to follow the beliefs that my father has that if you think there is a danger to our society you should do something. And I don't want to be involved with this stuff but I just want to try to offer context sometimes because I think that is hard to understand what this movement is and how somebody could be a part of this movement and also offer that perspective of how you can realize you're doing something really bad.

M.B.: *Sounds like you're following your father's beliefs, just not the way he intended for you.*

D.B.: I don't know if he sees it that way, but sometimes I do.

M.B.: *Derek, Thank you very, very much I really appreciate that.*

D.B.: Thanks.

M.B.: *Bye.*

Renouncing Hate: What Happens When a White Nationalist Repents

ESSAY | BY WES ENZINNA | SEPT. 10, 2018

AMERICANS LOVE REDEMPTION stories. The Old Testament tale of Exodus — the slaves' flight from Egypt and their salvation in the desert — may be the most epic of all such sagas, and the Puritans aboard the Mayflower thought of their flight from King James as an exodus of the chosen people fleeing their pharaoh. Ben Franklin's best-selling "Autobiography" mythologized his rags-to-riches rise from indentured servant to inventor and statesman, and in so doing he further stitched the redemption narrative into the nation's moral fabric. Since then, activists, politicians and businessmen have all borrowed the story line to lend legitimacy to their ambitions, but few have done so more powerfully than civil rights leaders: Martin Luther King Jr. insisted that Christians who had succumbed to bigotry could repent only by righting racial wrongs; Malcolm X recounted his transformation from hustler and felon to militant activist and Muslim, and in so doing, he invited a nation of sinners to follow him down the same spiritual path. In America, the resurrected wretch ("I once was lost but now am found") has more authority than the pious innocent — to have fallen and been redeemed is an act of self-invention and moral fortitude that mirrors the Pilgrims' own impossible journey.

Today, in the upside-down world that is Trump's America, where anything seems possible and nothing is off limits, we're seeing the emergence of a new type of redemption story: that of the white supremacist turned antiracist crusader. In defiance of antifa radicals who support "punching Nazis" to shut them up, and free-speech absolutists who think it's enough to ignore them and hope they'll go away, "formers," as many ex-white supremacists call themselves, teach us from their own experiences about the complicated roles empathy and exclusion play in conversion; about the addictive nature of hate; about how encounters with "others" can be transformative. "There will be people who will say, 'Once a Nazi, always a Nazi,' and that you can't change who you are," the former extremist Christian Picciolini says on a recent MSNBC special, "Breaking Hate," in which he coaches white supremacists trying to leave hate groups. "But I know change is possible."

In this vein comes **RISING OUT OF HATRED: The Awakening of a Former White Nationalist (Doubleday, $26.95),** by Eli Saslow, a Pulitzer Prize-winning reporter for The Washington Post, who tells the story of Derek Black, the son of Don Black, the founder of Stormfront, until recently the largest and most important extremist website in America. Derek's godfather is David Duke, the former Ku Klux Klan grand wizard and Louisiana state representative, who groomed Derek from an early age to succeed him as a leader of the white nationalist movement, and who saw in Derek's polite and thoughtful demeanor, his careful avoidance of racial slurs, his "shoulder-length red hair" and "large black cowboy hat," the precocious face of that future.

Saslow had full access to Derek, his father (who remains a committed white nationalist), and Derek's friends and acquaintances, who provided Saslow with invaluable chat logs, emails and recordings that allowed him to dramatize his subject's evolving belief system with novelistic intimacy. Derek and today's white nationalist movement matured alongside each other, and he learned from a young age that the old-school extremism practiced by his father was a liability. Before launching Stormfront in 1996, Don Black led the Alabama Ku Klux Klan and went to prison for plotting to overthrow the Caribbean island of Dominica in order to establish a white ethno-state there. Intuitive and whip-smart, young Derek learned from his father's failures that "white nationalism could only grow into a viable political movement if it adopted a new language of its own — a vocabulary that sanitized the ideology and distanced it from a history of violence."

JASON HENRY FOR THE NEW YORK TIMES

Derek Black and his father, Don, recording their radio show in 2011.

Growing up in West Palm Beach, Fla., he created a "kids" section of Stormfront aimed at recruiting "white children of the globe" and another one devoted to "The Lord of the Rings." He also co-hosted with his father a popular radio show that mixed country music with ideology. Seizing on a spike in interest in the site after Barack Obama became president, Derek persuaded his dad to ban racial slurs, Nazi imagery and threats of violence or lawbreaking, which helped the site grow from 30,000 users in 2007 to 300,000 in 2017. "You've laid the foundation to build our new white republic," Matthew Heimbach, a young white nationalist leader, told Don Black and a crowd of white supremacists in Tennessee in 2013. "Now my generation is primed for this revolution. ... I've been reading Stormfront since I was in high school, and it planted the seeds in my mind."

By that time, however, Derek had undergone a transformation. In 2010, he enrolled at New College of Florida, in Sarasota, where his dad was convinced he was on a reconnaissance mission, living, as a caller to their radio show put it, "among the enemy in a hotbed of multiculturalism." Instead, Derek made fast friends with Juan, a Peruvian immigrant, and Matthew, an Orthodox Jew, and he dated a Jewish woman named Rose, feeling "as if he were occupying two lives: breakfast at New College with Rose and one of her transgender friends and then Thanksgiving dinner with Don, Chloe" — Derek's mother — "and a few former skinheads in West Palm Beach."

The more academic life grew on Derek, the more he feared that his peers would discover his alter ego, and one night in the spring of his first year that's exactly what happened. On a campuswide online message board, someone posted a photo of Black: "Have you seen this man? Derek Black. White supremacist, radio host ... New College student?"

Saslow has a knack for milking his characters' trials for all their zeitgeisty relevance, and he shows how the resulting conflict between students and administrators foreshadowed larger questions that campuses across the country would soon confront about free speech and extremism. At one point after being exposed, Derek ventured out during a campus festival and was heckled by fellow students. Another day, a student, posting on the schoolwide online forum, declared: "Violence against white supremacists will send a message that white supremacists will get beat up. That's very productive."

Yet while most students shunned Derek, Matthew refused to do so. As an observant Jew, he had "already experienced enough shaming at New College to believe that exclusion only reinforced divides," and he continued to invite Derek to Shabbat dinners, which on any given night might include a few Orthodox Jews, an immigrant and a gay student. But when, after months of these dinners, Derek failed to transform from a white nationalist caterpillar into a progressive butterfly — at one point he even organized a high-profile conference of white nationalist leaders — his friends confronted a strategic and moral conflict that mirrors the plight of many Americans today when deciding how best to deal with racists. As Moshe, a friend, whose grandfather survived the Bergen-Belsen concentration camp, wondered: "What if all he had done by befriending Derek was to enable him, to provide him with cover from the social-justice activists on campus so that he could continue to promote a racist ideology while living a comfortable college life? What incentive did Derek have to change?"

His incentive, it would turn out, was romantic love. At the dinners he met a woman named Allison who at first gave him the cold shoulder and then justified her inexplicable attraction to him as being part of a project to reform him, though in reality her feelings for Derek were as organic — and confusing — for her as they were for him.

As Allison grew to love Derek, and as he reciprocated, he began to trust her. Christian Picciolini, in his memoir, "White American Youth" (2017), describes the importance of empathy — how receiving it from others at a time when he felt he least deserved it was lifesaving, helping to pull him out of extremism. But the importance of empathy is primarily that it builds trust, and once you trust someone, you'll listen to him or her. For Derek, that meant listening to Allison when she sent him dozens of studies over the course of many months showing, for example, that victims of racism had higher blood pressure, depression and heart disease. "For years Derek had been hearing about the abstract evils of racism, which he had always dismissed as empty rhetoric from his enemies on the liberal left," Saslow writes. But Allison "made Derek begin to wonder if in fact he had been wrong in his theory that actually it was white people who were discriminated against."

Allison also forced him to imagine the effects his ideas would have on people he cared about at New College. One weekend, while the two were driving back to school from a road trip to a state park, a relationship spat turned into a full-on ideological battle. Even though Derek had by now begun privately doubting many of his beliefs, he still clung to the idea that white nationalism was simply about defending whites, not harming nonwhites. "Your stupid theory makes no sense," Allison finally said. "Didn't white nationalists want to deport ... minorities and uproot their lives? ... Did he somehow not understand why that idea would be threatening for Rose, or Moshe or Matthew? ... When the great deportation came, would Derek himself be willing to break into their homes and force them out? Or would he stand by and watch as his father and other Stormfront members did it for him?"

When Derek later confronts his dad with this same question, at least Don is honest about the implications of what he'd been advocating all along: Immigrants, Jews and blacks could "be forced to leave," he replies, to Derek's horror. "This country is on the verge of a reckoning." Derek's naïveté, on the other hand, is exasperating, and by the time he finally tells Allison, in his senior year, "I'm done. I don't believe in it, and I'm not going to be involved," it's a bit anticlimactic.

It may be impossible to trace a direct connection between Derek's beliefs and activities, on the one hand, and white nationalist violence, on the other. But it's a discomfiting fact that at least six murderers turn out to have used Stormfront as a resource, including Dylann Roof, who logged on as "LilAryan" before killing nine African-American churchgoers in Charleston in 2015. In his 23 years as a white nationalist, Derek gave dozens of interviews and speeches, and organized a large conference promoting his ideas; his radio show influenced hundreds, possibly thousands of people.

By the time Trump became the Republican nominee for president, Derek had changed his name to Roland Derek Black, quit the movement, been disowned by some members of his family and enrolled in a Ph.D. program in medieval history at the University of Chicago. He wanted to hide — he was disgusted with himself — but Allison, ever his moral compass, insisted that he owed a debt to the country he helped divide. Like his dad and David Duke, Derek saw in Trump's rise a validation of their efforts to popularize white nationalism, though unlike them he was aghast. "Maybe Trump wasn't in fact a white nationalist," Don cheers, "but he sure was good at sounding like one."

Yet when Derek finally decides to go all out in denouncing white nationalism in an Op-Ed in The New York Times, becoming a reluctant public face of antiracism days after the election, the reader can't help feeling that he's getting off, and out of the movement, a little too easily. In Picciolini's case, his wife and children left him and he sank into a suicidal depression before his rebirth as a "former"; Frank Meeink, the ex-Nazi author of "Autobiography of a Recovering Skinhead," became addicted to heroin; and Angela King, the subject of "Meeting a Monster," a recent biopic about her life as a skinhead, went to prison. As any reader of the Bible knows, the more dramatic the suffering, the more rewarding the redemption, and in the end, Derek Black's transformation is too little, too late. At the conclusion of "Rising Out of Hatred," he's a student in a top Ph.D. program and gets to keep the girl, while his parents threaten only to take away his credit card.

"I'm part of all this, and it makes me ill," he told Allison in the summer of 2016, a few months before Trump's election. "I wish there was some way to not think about that."

WES ENZINNA is a senior editor at Harper's.

A Voice of Hate in America's Heartland

BY RICHARD FAUSSET | NOV. 25, 2017

HUBER HEIGHTS, OHIO — Tony and Maria Hovater were married this fall. They registered at Target. On their list was a muffin pan, a four-drawer dresser and a pineapple slicer.

Ms. Hovater, 25, was worried about Antifa bashing up the ceremony. Weddings are hard enough to plan for when your fiancé is not an avowed white nationalist.

But Mr. Hovater, in the days leading up to the wedding, was somewhat less anxious. There are times when it can feel toxic to openly identify as a far-right extremist in the Ohio of 2017. But not always. He said the election of President Trump helped open a space for people like him, demonstrating that it is not the end of the world to be attacked as the bigot he surely is: "You can just say, 'Yeah, so?' And move on."

It was a weeknight at Applebee's in Huber Heights, a suburb of Dayton, a few weeks before the wedding. The couple, who live in nearby New Carlisle, were shoulder to shoulder at a table, young and in love. He was in a plain T-shirt, she in a sleeveless jean jacket. She ordered the boneless wings. Her parents had met him, she said, and approved of the match. The wedding would be small. Some of her best friends were going to be there. "A lot of girls are not really into politics," she said.

In Ohio, amid the row crops and rolling hills, the Olive Gardens and Steak 'n Shakes, Mr. Hovater's presence can make hardly a ripple. He is the Nazi sympathizer next door, polite and low-key at a time the old boundaries of accepted political activity can seem alarmingly in flux. Most Americans would be disgusted and baffled by his casually approving remarks about Hitler, disdain for democracy and belief that the races are better off separate. But his tattoos are innocuous pop-culture references: a slice of cherry pie adorns one arm, a homage to the TV show "Twin Peaks." He says he prefers to spread the gospel of white nationalism with satire. He is a big "Seinfeld" fan.

GEORGE ETHEREDGE FOR THE NEW YORK TIMES

Tony Hovater at his home in New Carlisle, Ohio.

"I guess it seems weird when talking about these type of things," he says. "You know, I'm coming at it in a mid-90s, Jewish, New York, observational-humor way."

Mr. Hovater, 29, is a welder by trade. He is not a star among the resurgent radical American right so much as a committed foot soldier — an organizer, an occasional podcast guest on a website called Radio Aryan, and a self-described "social media villain," although, in person, his Midwestern manners would please anyone's mother. In 2015, he helped start the Traditionalist Worker Party, one of the extreme right-wing groups that marched in Charlottesville, Va., in August, and again at a "White Lives Matter" rally last month in Tennessee. The group's stated mission is to "fight for the interests of White Americans."

Its leaders claim to oppose racism, though the Anti-Defamation League says the group "has participated in white supremacist events all over the country." On its website, a swastika armband goes for $20.

If the Charlottesville rally came as a shock, with hundreds of white

Americans marching in support of ideologies many have long considered too vile, dangerous or stupid to enter the political mainstream, it obscured the fact that some in the small, loosely defined alt-right movement are hoping to make those ideas seem less than shocking for the "normies," or normal people, that its sympathizers have tended to mock online.

And to go from mocking to wooing, the movement will be looking to make use of people like the Hovaters and their trappings of normie life — their fondness for National Public Radio, their four cats, their bridal registry.

"We need to have more families. We need to be able to just be normal," said Matthew Heimbach, the leader of the Traditionalist Worker Party, in a podcast conversation with Mr. Hovater. Why, he asked self-mockingly, were so many followers "abnormal"?

Mr. Hovater replied: "I mean honestly, it takes people with, like, sort of an odd view of life, at first, to come this way. Because most people are pacified really easy, you know. Like, here's some money, here's a nice TV, go watch your sports, you know?"

He added: "The fact that we're seeing more and more normal people come is because things have gotten so bad. And if they keep getting worse, we'll keep getting more, just, normal people."

FLATTENING THE EDGES

Mr. Hovater's face is narrow and punctuated with sharply peaked eyebrows, like a pair of air quotes, and he tends to deliver his favorite adjective, "edgy," with a flat affect and maximum sarcastic intent. It is a sort of implicit running assertion that the edges of acceptable American political discourse — edges set by previous generations, like the one that fought the Nazis — are laughable.

"I don't want you to think I'm some 'edgy' Republican," he says, while flatly denouncing the concept of democracy.

"I don't even think those things should be 'edgy,' " he says, while defending his assertion that Jews run the worlds of finance and the media, and "appear to be working more in line with their own interests than everybody else's."

His political evolution — from vaguely leftist rock musician to ardent libertarian to fascist activist — was largely fueled by the kinds of frustrations that would not seem exotic to most American conservatives. He believes the federal government is too big, the news media is biased, and that affirmative action programs for minorities are fundamentally unfair.

Ask him how he moved so far right, and he declares that public discourse has become "so toxic that there's no way to effectively lobby for interests that involve white people." He name-drops Murray Rothbard and Hans-Hermann Hoppe, architects of "anarcho-capitalism," with its idea that free markets serve as better societal regulators than the state. And he refers to the 2013 science-fiction movie "Pacific Rim," in which society is attacked by massive monsters that emerge from beneath the Pacific Ocean.

GEORGE ETHEREDGE FOR THE NEW YORK TIMES

A bookshelf at Mr. Hovater's house.

"So the people, they don't ask the monsters to stop," he says. "They build a giant robot to try to stop them. And that's essentially what fascism is. It's like our version of centrally coming together to try to stop another already centralized force."

Mr. Hovater grew up on integrated Army bases and attended a mostly white Ohio high school. He did not want for anything. He experienced no scarring racial episodes. His parents, he says, were the kinds of people who "always assume things aren't going well. But they don't necessarily know why."

He is adamant that the races are probably better off separated, but he insists he is not racist. He is a white nationalist, he says, not a white supremacist. There were mixed-race couples at the wedding. Mr. Hovater said he was fine with it.

"That's their thing, man," he said.

Online it is uglier. On Facebook, Mr. Hovater posted a picture purporting to show what life would have looked like if Germany had won World War II: a streetscape full of happy white people, a bustling American-style diner and swastikas everywhere.

"What part is supposed to look unappealing?" he wrote.

In an essay lamenting libertarianism's leftward drift, he wrote: "At this rate I'm sure the presidential candidate they'll put up in a few cycles will be an overweight, black, crippled dyke with dyslexia."

After he attended the Charlottesville rally, in which a white nationalist plowed his car into a group of left-wing protesters, killing one of them, Mr. Hovater wrote that he was proud of the comrades who joined him there: "We made history. Hail victory."

In German, "Hail victory" is "Sieg heil."

A GROWING MOVEMENT

Before white nationalism, his world was heavy metal. He played drums in two bands, and his embrace of fascism, on the surface, shares some traits with the hipster's cooler-than-thou quest for the most extreme of musical subgenres. Online, he and his allies can also give the impression that their movement is one big laugh — an enormous trolling event put on by self-mocking, politically incorrect kids playing around on the ash heap of history.

On the party's website, the swastika armband is formally listed as a "NSDAP LARP Armband." NSDAP was the abbreviation for Hitler's Nazi Party. LARP stands for "Live-Action Role Playing," a term originally meant to describe fantasy fans who dress up as wizards and warlocks.

But the movement is no joke. The party, Mr. Hovater said, is now approaching 1,000 people. He said that it has held food and school-supply drives in Appalachia. "These are people that the establishment doesn't care about," he said.

Marilyn Mayo, a senior research fellow at the Anti-Defamation League's Center on Extremism, estimated that the Traditionalist Worker Party had a few hundred members at most, while Americans who identify as "alt-right" could number in the tens of thousands.

"It is small in the grand scheme of things, but it's one of the segments of the white supremacist movement that's grown over the last two years," she said.

It was midday at a Panera Bread, and Mr. Hovater was describing his political awakening over a turkey sandwich. He mentioned books by Charles Murray and Pat Buchanan. He talked about his presence on 4chan, the online message board and alt-right breeding ground ("That's where the scary memes come from," he deadpanned). He spoke dispassionately about the injustice of affirmative action, about the "malice directed toward white people" in popular media, about how the cartoon comedy "King of the Hill" was the last TV show to portray "a straight white male patriarch" in a positive light.

He declared the widely accepted estimate that six million Jews died in the Holocaust "overblown." He said that while the Nazi leader Heinrich Himmler wanted to exterminate groups like Slavs and homosexuals, Hitler "was a lot more kind of chill on those subjects."

GEORGE ETHEREDGE FOR THE NEW YORK TIMES

Mr. Hovater and others in the loosely defined alt-right movement are hoping to make their ideas less than shocking, even normal.

"I think he was a guy who really believed in his cause," he said of Hitler. "He really believed he was fighting for his people and doing what he thought was right."

He said he wanted to see the United States become "an actually fair, meritocratic society." Absent that, he would settle for a white ethnostate "where things are fair, because there's no competing demographics for government power or for resources."

His fascist ideal, he said, would resemble the early days in the United States, when power was reserved for landowners "and, you know, normies didn't really have a whole hell of a lot to say."

His faith in mainstream solutions slipped as he toured the country with one of the metal bands. "I got to see people who were genuinely hurting," he said. "We played coast to coast, but specifically places in Appalachia, and a lot of the Eastern Seaboard had really been hurt."

FRIENDSHIPS MADE AND LOST

In 2012, Mr. Hovater was incensed by the media coverage of the Trayvon Martin shooting, believing the story had been distorted to make a villain of George Zimmerman, the white man who shot the black teenager. By that time, he and Ms. Hovater had been dating for a year or two. She was a small-town girl who had fallen away from the Catholic Church ("It was just really boring"), and once considered herself liberal.

But in the aftermath of the shooting, Ms. Hovater found herself on social media "questioning the official story," taking Mr. Zimmerman's side and finding herself blocked by some of her friends. Today, she says, she and Mr. Hovater are "pretty lined up" politically.

As they let their views be known, friends left and friends stayed.

"His views are horrible and repugnant and hate-filled," said Ethan Reynolds, a Republican and city councilman in New Carlisle, Ohio, who said he had befriended Mr. Hovater without knowing his extremism. "He was an acquaintance I regret knowing."

Jake Nolan, a guitarist in one of the bands Mr. Hovater played in, stuck with him. "There are people who literally go around Sieg Heiling," he said. "Then you have the people who just want the right to be proud of their heritage" — people, he said, who are standing up against "what appears to be an increasingly anti-white America."

Mr. Hovater befriended Mr. Heimbach in February 2015 at the Conservative Political Action Conference. Mr. Heimbach, who two years earlier had founded a White Student Union at Towson University in Maryland, was holding a protest outside the proceedings and praising Vladimir Putin. The pair founded the Traditionalist Worker Party in the spring.

Soon Mr. Hovater was telling people that he would be running for a council seat in his hometown, New Carlisle, population 5,600. The announcement caught the attention of the Southern Poverty Law Center and the heavy metal press. But he never filed papers.

On a recent weekday evening, Mr. Hovater was at home, sautéing minced garlic with chili flakes and waiting for his pasta to boil. The cats were wandering in and out of their tidy little rental house. Books about Mussolini and Hitler shared shelf space with a stack of Nintendo Wii games. A day earlier, a next-door neighbor, whom Mr. Hovater doesn't know very well, had hung a Confederate flag in front of his house.

"This is kind of brackish territory here," Mr. Hovater said. "A lot of people consider Cincinnati the most northern Southern city."

The pasta was ready. Ms. Hovater talked about how frightening it was this summer to watch from home as the Charlottesville rally spun out of control. Mr. Hovater said he was glad the movement had grown.

They spoke about their future — about moving to a bigger place, about their honeymoon, about having kids.

I Interviewed a White Nationalist and Fascist. What Was I Left With?

BY RICHARD FAUSSET | NOV. 25, 2017

THERE IS A HOLE at the heart of my story about Tony Hovater, the white nationalist and Nazi sympathizer.

Why did this man — intelligent, socially adroit and raised middle class amid the relatively well-integrated environments of United States military bases — gravitate toward the furthest extremes of American political discourse?

I had hoped the answer would fall in my lap when I traveled to Ohio to spend time with Mr. Hovater. We met at a Panera Bread, at his suggestion. We ate turkey sandwiches. At my prompting, he described his life growing up, a life that seemed altogether unremarkable. He spoke of a number of moments that soured him on mainstream politics, none of them particularly exotic. One was the Republican National Committee's rule changes, during the 2012 convention, that worked against Mr. Hovater's preferred candidate at the time, the libertarian Ron Paul, and in favor of Mitt Romney, the eventual Republican nominee. Mr. Hovater called it "the first time I thought about how a system will protect itself, and its own interests, to protect what it is they really want."

He talked about his time as a heavy metal drummer, though he said he was not particularly drawn to the transgressive promises of the genre. His father, after all, was a Black Sabbath fan. Mr. Hovater was more interested in the technical challenge of the music.

And yet what, of any of this, explained Mr. Hovater's radical turn? What prompted him to take his ideas beyond his living room, beyond the chat rooms, and on to Charlottesville, where he marched in August alongside allies like the neo-Confederate League of the South and the Detroit-based National Socialist Movement, which bills itself as "America's Premier White Civil Rights Organization"? Where was his Rosebud?

After I had filed an early version of the article, an editor at The Times told me he felt like the question had not been sufficiently addressed. So I went back to Mr. Hovater in search of answers. I still don't think I really found them. I could feel the failure even as Mr. Hovater and I spoke on the phone, adding to what had already been hours of face-to-face conversation in and around his hometown New Carlisle, Ohio.

On the phone, Mr. Hovater responded to my question by rattling off names of libertarian academics, making references to sci-fi movies and describing, yet again, his frustration with what he described as the plodding and unjust nature of American democracy. As he did so, I was thinking about an album I grew up with by the Minutemen, the Southern California punk group, and its brilliantly koanic title: "What Makes a Man Start Fires?"

To me, that question embodies what good journalism should strive for, as well as the limits of the enterprise. Sometimes all we can bring you is the words of the police spokesman, the suspect's picture from a high school yearbook, the acrid stench of the burned woods.

Sometimes a soul, and its shape, remain obscure to both writer and reader.

I beat myself up about all of this for a while, until I decided that the unfilled hole would have to serve as both feature and defect. What I had were quotidian details, though to be honest, I'm not even sure what these add up to. Like other committed extremists I have known, Mr. Hovater had little time for a life beyond his full-time job and his line of activism. When he is not doing those things, he likes to be at home with his girlfriend (now his wife) and their cats.

Mr. Hovater was exceedingly candid with me — often shockingly so — but it seems as though his worldview was largely formed by the same recombinant stuff that influences our mainstream politics. There were exceptions, of course: I saw, on his bookshelf, two volumes of Helena Blavatsky's "The Secret Doctrine," a 19th-century work of esoteric spiritualism whose anti-Semitism influenced Nazi thinking.

But even if I had called Mr. Hovater yet again — even if we had discussed Blavatsky at length, the way we did his ideas about the Federal Reserve Bank — I'm not sure it would have answered the question.

What makes a man start fires?

Readers Accuse Us of Normalizing a Nazi Sympathizer; We Respond

BY MARC LACEY | NOV. 26, 2017

We have asked our national editor, Marc Lacey, to respond to feedback on our recent profile of a white nationalist.

A PROFILE IN The Times of Tony Hovater, a white nationalist and Nazi sympathizer in Ohio, elicited a huge amount of feedback this weekend, most of it sharply critical. Here's how the piece came about, why we wrote it and why we think it was important to do so.

The genesis of the story was the aftermath of the white supremacist rally in Charlottesville, Va., in August, the terrifying Ku Klux Klan-like images of young white men carrying tiki torches and shouting "Jews will not replace us," and the subsequent violence that included the killing of a woman, Heather D. Heyer.

Who were those people? We assigned Richard Fausset, one of our smartest thinkers and best writers, to profile one of the far-right foot soldiers at the rally. We ended up settling on Mr. Hovater, who, it turned out, was a few years older than another Ohio man, James Alex Fields Jr., who was charged with murder after the authorities said he drove his car into a crowd of protesters, killing Ms. Heyer.

Our reporter went to Ohio to spend time with Mr. Hovater and submitted several drafts and updates in between assignments that included Hurricane Harvey in Houston, Hurricane Maria in Puerto Rico and the Roy Moore campaign in Alabama. The story finally ran online Saturday.

Whatever our goal, a lot of readers found the story offensive, with many seizing on the idea we were normalizing neo-Nazi views and behavior. "How to normalize Nazis 101!" one reader wrote on Twitter. "I'm both shocked and disgusted by this article," wrote another. "Attempting to 'normalize' white supremacist groups — should Never have been printed!"

Our reporter and his editors agonized over the tone and content of the article. The point of the story was not to normalize anything but to describe the degree to which hate and extremism have become far more normal in American life than many of us want to think.

We described Mr. Hovater as a bigot, a Nazi sympathizer who posted images on Facebook of a Nazi-like America full of happy white people and swastikas everywhere.

We understand that some readers wanted more pushback, and we hear that loud and clear.

Some readers also criticized the article for including a link to a webpage that sells swastika armbands. This was intended to show the darker reality beyond the anodyne language of the website. But we saw the criticism, agreed and removed the link.

Some readers did see value in the piece. Shane Bauer, a senior reporter at Mother Jones and a winner of the National Magazine Award, tweeted: "People mad about this article want to believe that Nazis are monsters we cannot relate to. White supremacists are normal ass white people and it's been that way in America since 1776. We will continue to be in trouble till we understand that."

But far more were outraged by the article. "You know who had nice manners?" Bess Kalb, a writer for Jimmy Kimmel Live, said on Twitter. "The Nazi who shaved my uncle Willie's head before escorting him into a cement chamber where he locked eyes with children as their lungs filled with poison and they suffocated to death in agony. Too much? Exactly. That's how you write about Nazis."

Others urged us to focus our journalism less on those pushing hate and more on those on the receiving end of that hate. "Instead of long, glowing profiles of Nazis/White nationalists, why don't we profile the victims of their ideologies?" asked Karen Attiah, an editor at The Washington Post. "Why not a piece about the mother of Heather Heyer, the woman who was killed in Charlottesville? Follow-ups on those who were injured? Or how PoC are coping?"

We regret the degree to which the piece offended so many readers.

We recognize that people can disagree on how best to tell a disagreeable story. What we think is indisputable, though, is the need to shed more light, not less, on the most extreme corners of American life and the people who inhabit them. That's what the story, however imperfectly, tried to do.

As always, we want to continue hearing from our readers. Please share your thoughts in the comments. We will be reading them.

CHAPTER 4

White Nationalism and Politics

In 2016, Donald Trump embraced incendiary rhetoric on the campaign trail, even going so far as to identify as a nationalist. Upon his election, white nationalist groups celebrated: In the president-elect, they saw someone who shared their vision of a white homeland. Since Trump's election, white nationalists have begun to feature more prominently in the national discourse. The articles in this chapter explore how their presence has been felt on a national stage.

White Nationalists Celebrate 'an Awakening' After Donald Trump's Victory

BY ALAN RAPPEPORT AND NOAH WEILAND | NOV. 19, 2016

WASHINGTON — For years, they have lurked in the web's dark corners, masking themselves with cartoon images and writing screeds about the demise of white culture under ominous pseudonyms. But on Saturday, in the wake of Donald J. Trump's surprising election victory, hundreds of his extremist supporters converged on the capital to herald a moment of political ascendance that many had thought to be far away.

In the bowels of the Ronald Reagan Building and International Trade Center, three blocks from the White House, members of the so-called alt-right movement gathered for what they had supposed would be an autopsy to plot their grim future under a Clinton administration. Instead, they celebrated the unexpected march of their white nationalist ideas toward the mainstream, portraying Mr. Trump's win as validation that the tide had turned in their fight to preserve white culture.

"It's been an awakening," Richard B. Spencer, who is credited with coining the term alt-right, said at the gathering on Saturday. "This is what a successful movement looks like."

The movement has been critical of politicians of all stripes for promoting diversity, immigration and perceived political correctness. Its critics call it a rebranded version of the Ku Klux Klan, promoting anti-Semitism, violence and suppression of minorities.

Intellectual leaders of the movement argue that they are merely trying to realize their desire for a white "ethno-state" where they can be left alone. Mr. Trump, with his divisive language about immigrants and Muslims, has given them hope that these dreams can come true.

"I never thought we would get to this point, any point close to mainstream acceptance or political influence," said Matt Forney, 28, of Chicago. "The culture is moving more in my direction."

Emboldened by Mr. Trump's takeover of the Republican Party, Mr. Forney said he expected people openly associated with the white nationalist movement to run as candidates in the 2018 midterm elections. The rise of populism and the decline of political correctness, he said, present a rare opportunity.

Robert Taylor, 29, described the conference as a "victory party." Mr. Taylor was a committed libertarian, he said, working for Ron Paul's presidential campaigns and even moving to New Hampshire for a project organized by the like-minded. If Hillary Clinton had won the election, he said, he would have advocated secession.

"I thought I had all the right answers and had read all the right books," he said. "I heard about the alt-right movement, and it just lit a fire in me."

Mr. Taylor said that with Mr. Trump, "we have breathing room; we have a little time."

AL DRAGO/THE NEW YORK TIMES

Richard B. Spencer, a leader of the far right, addressing a conference on Saturday in Washington.

Mr. Trump has shrugged off any suggestions that he has connections to the alt-right. But his hard-line views on immigration and his "America First" foreign policy have captivated members of the movement. His appointment as chief strategist of Stephen K. Bannon, who has called Breitbart News, the website he long ran, a platform for the alt-right, has reinforced the notion that the incoming president is on their side.

The white nationalist embrace of Mr. Trump was on display Saturday at the gathering, which was the annual conference of a group called the National Policy Institute. Guests nibbled on chicken piccata while discussing ways to reorient America's demographics. Many of the attendees, who were mostly white men, wore red "Make America Great Again" hats. T-shirts emblazoned with Mr. Trump's face sold quickly.

While the enthusiasm inside the conference was evident, the resistance to the alt-right remains powerful. A recent surge in hate crimes and reports of verbal and physical assaults on minorities are putting new pressure on groups that promote racism.

Many sites will not host their events, and some of their members have had their social media accounts suspended in response to vicious trolling of Jewish journalists and critics of Mr. Trump. A large group of protesters marched around the Ronald Reagan Building, which, as a federal property, could not decline to host the conference.

"These people have their right to freedom of speech, but the values they represent don't represent America," said Jon Pattee, 48. "I characterize them as the shirt-and-tie arm of the white supremacist-nationalist movement."

Republicans who are more mainstream are also unlikely to accept the movement's more provocative ideas.

"They have to grow up and start shedding some of their more controversial elements," said Erick Erickson, a conservative blogger and commentator who has been critical of Mr. Trump. "I don't think they will ever be accepted wholeheartedly in the Republican Party."

Nonetheless, alt-right leaders said they planned to use their newfound influence to pressure Mr. Trump to take more "heretical" policy positions, such as a moratorium on net immigration for the next 50 years. White Europeans, Mr. Spencer said, would be given preference.

"In the long run, people like Bannon and Trump will be open to the clarity of our ideas," said Jared Taylor, the founder of the white nationalist publication American Renaissance.

Like Mr. Trump, Mr. Spencer, who has become the face of the alt-right, derided NATO as "clumsy and ineffective." He called for friendlier relations with the Russian president, Vladimir V. Putin, and for the deportation of undocumented immigrants, drawing chants of "build that wall."

"I think moving forward the alt-right as an intellectual vanguard can complete Trump," Mr. Spencer said. "We can be the ones who are out front, who are thinking about things that he hasn't grasped yet."

Although alt-right leaders say they want to become more politically active, it remains unclear how they will react to being more closely aligned to the establishment or what they will do if Mr. Trump starts to moderate his views. His outreach to African-Americans during the final months of the campaign angered some of his white nationalist followers, raising concerns among them that Mr. Trump might not be so different after all.

"It's a fleeting moment of optimism," said Al Stankard, 29, of Baltimore, who goes by the pseudonym Haarlen Venison online and was handing out his novel, "Death to the World."

Mr. Stankard said he thought it was unlikely that Mr. Trump would be able to do things like end affirmative action, even though he believes that the president-elect sympathizes with the plight of "white racists." He predicted that Mr. Trump might disappoint white nationalists in the same way that President Obama disappointed some of his supporters by failing to bring postracial unity to the nation.

"These are semi-delusional fantasies," Mr. Stankard said.

Alt-Right Gathering Exults in Trump Election With Nazi-Era Salute

BY JOSEPH GOLDSTEIN | NOV. 20, 2016

WASHINGTON — By the time Richard B. Spencer, the leading ideologue of the alt-right movement and the final speaker of the night, rose to address a gathering of his followers on Saturday, the crowd was restless.

In 11 hours of speeches and panel discussions in a federal building named after Ronald Reagan a few blocks from the White House, a succession of speakers had laid out a harsh vision for the future, but had denounced violence and said that Hispanic citizens and black Americans had nothing to fear. Earlier in the day, Mr. Spencer himself had urged the group to start acting less like an underground organization and more like the establishment.

But now his tone changed as he began to tell the audience of more than 200 people, mostly young men, what they had been waiting to hear. He railed against Jews and, with a smile, quoted Nazi propaganda in the original German. America, he said, belonged to white people, whom he called the "children of the sun," a race of conquerors and creators who had been marginalized but now, in the era of President-elect Donald J. Trump, were "awakening to their own identity." As he finished, several audience members had their arms outstretched in a Nazi salute. Mr. Spencer called out: "Hail Trump! Hail our people!" and then, "Hail victory!" — the English translation of the Nazi exhortation "Sieg Heil!" The room shouted back.

These are exultant times for the alt-right movement, which was little known until this year, when it embraced Mr. Trump's campaign and he appeared to embrace it back. He chose as his campaign chairman Stephen K. Bannon, the media executive who ran the alt-right's most prominent platform, Breitbart News, and then named him as a senior adviser and chief strategist.

Now the movement's leaders hope to have, if not a seat at the table, at least the ear of the Trump White House.

While many of its racist views are well known — that President Obama is, or may as well be, of foreign birth; that the Black Lives Matter movement is another name for black race rioters; that even the American-born children of undocumented Hispanic immigrants should be deported — the alt-right has been difficult to define. Is it a name for right-wing political provocateurs in the internet era? Or is it a political movement defined by xenophobia and a dislike for political correctness?

At the conference on Saturday, Mr. Spencer, who said he had coined the term, defined the alt-right as a movement with white identity as its core idea.

"We've crossed the Rubicon in terms of recognition," Mr. Spencer said at the conference, which was sponsored by his organization, the National Policy Institute.

And while much of the discourse at the conference was overtly racist and demeaning toward minorities, for much of the day the sentiments were expressed in ways that seemed intended to not sound too menacing. The focus was on how whites were marginalized and beleaguered.

One speaker, Peter Brimelow, the founder of Vdare.com, an anti-immigration website, asked why, if Hispanics had the National Council of La Raza and Jews had the Anti-Defamation League, whites were reluctant to organize for their rights. Some speakers made an effort to distance themselves from more notorious white power organizations like the Ku Klux Klan.

But as the night wore on and most reporters had gone home, the language changed.

Mr. Spencer's after-dinner speech began with a polemic against the "mainstream media," before he briefly paused. "Perhaps we should refer to them in the original German?" he said.

The audience immediately screamed back, "Lügenpresse," reviving a Nazi-era word that means "lying press."

Mr. Spencer suggested that the news media had been critical of Mr. Trump throughout the campaign in order to protect Jewish interests. He mused about the political commentators who gave Mr. Trump little chance of winning.

"One wonders if these people are people at all, or instead soulless golem," he said, referring to a Jewish fable about the golem, a clay giant that a rabbi brings to life to protect the Jews.

Mr. Trump's election, Mr. Spencer said, was "the victory of will," a phrase that echoed the title of the most famous Nazi-era propaganda film. But Mr. Spencer then mentioned, with a smile, Theodor Herzl, the Zionist leader who advocated a Jewish homeland in Israel, quoting his famous pronouncement, "If we will it, it is no dream."

The United States today, Mr. Spencer said, had been turned into "a sick, corrupted society." But it was not supposed to be that way.

"America was, until this last generation, a white country designed for ourselves and our posterity," Mr. Spencer thundered. "It is our creation, it is our inheritance, and it belongs to us."

But the white race, he added, is "a race that travels forever on an upward path."

"To be white is to be a creator, an explorer, a conqueror," he said.

More members of the audience were on their feet as Mr. Spencer described the choice facing white people as to "conquer or die."

Of other races, Mr. Spencer said: "We don't exploit other groups, we don't gain anything from their presence. They need us, and not the other way around."

The ties between the alt-right movement and the Trump team are difficult to define, even by members of the alt-right.

Mr. Bannon was the chief executive of Breitbart, an online news organization that has fed the lie that Mr. Obama is a Kenyan-born Muslim. As recently as last year, Breitbart published an op-ed article urging that "every tree, every rooftop, every picket fence, every telegraph pole in the South should be festooned with the Confederate battle flag."

Mr. Bannon told Mother Jones this year that Breitbart was now "the platform for the alt-right."

But in an interview last week with The Wall Street Journal, Mr. Bannon said that the alt-right was only "a tiny part" of the viewpoint represented on Breitbart.

"Our definition of the alt-right is younger people who are anti-globalists, very nationalist, terribly anti-establishment," he told The Journal, adding that the alt-right had "some racial and anti-Semitic overtones."

When asked about Mr. Bannon, the conference's speakers said that they might have shaken his hand on occasion, but that they did not know him well.

Mr. Brimelow said that he had met "Mr. Bannon once, earlier this summer, before he ascended to Olympus." He said he had told Mr. Bannon that he was doing great work at Breitbart. "He agreed," Mr. Brimelow recalled to the audience.

As for Mr. Trump, Mr. Brimelow said he had met him about 30 years ago at a "conservative affinity meeting" in Manhattan. But that was it.

"Trump and Steve Bannon are not alt-right people," Mr. Brimelow said, adding that they had opportunistically seized on two issues that the alt-right cares most about — stopping immigration and fighting political correctness — and used them to mobilize white voters.

Mr. Spencer said that while he did not think the president-elect should be considered alt-right, "I do think we have a psychic connection, or you can say a deeper connection, with Donald Trump in a way that we simply do not have with most Republicans."

White identity, he said, is at the core of both the alt-right movement and the Trump movement, even if most voters for Mr. Trump "aren't willing to articulate it as such."

At various points, he and other speakers outlined where they differed from Mr. Trump. They see him as too beholden to Israel. They do not see any reason to start a trade war with China, and they are not necessarily opposed to the Iran nuclear deal.

For them, immigration is the most potent mobilizing issue, less for economic reasons than because of the prospect that white Americans will someday represent less than half of the population of the country.

For the alt-right, the most exciting thing about Mr. Trump was that he built a campaign around the issues that mattered most to them, and that white people had voted for him in numbers that left the political establishments of both parties stunned. Now, Mr. Spencer said, it is up to the alt-right to formulate the ideas and policies to guide the new administration.

"I think we can be the ones out in front, thinking about those things he hasn't quite grasped yet, who are putting forward policies," Mr. Spencer said, that "have a realistic chance of being implemented."

Trump Gives White Supremacists an Unequivocal Boost

BY GLENN THRUSH AND MAGGIE HABERMAN | AUG. 15, 2017

WASHINGTON — President Trump buoyed the white nationalist movement on Tuesday as no president has done in generations — equating activists protesting racism with the neo-Nazis and white supremacists who rampaged in Charlottesville, Va., over the weekend.

Never has he gone as far in defending their actions as he did during a wild, street-corner shouting match of a news conference in the gilded lobby of Trump Tower, angrily asserting that so-called alt-left activists were just as responsible for the bloody confrontation as marchers brandishing swastikas, Confederate battle flags, anti-Semitic banners and "Trump/Pence" signs.

"Thank you President Trump for your honesty & courage to tell the truth," David Duke, a former Ku Klux Klan leader, wrote in a Twitter post shortly after Mr. Trump spoke.

Richard B. Spencer, a white nationalist leader who participated in the weekend's demonstrations and vowed to flood Charlottesville with similar protests in the coming weeks, was equally encouraged. "Trump's statement was fair and down to earth," Mr. Spencer tweeted.

Gov. Terry McAuliffe of Virginia, a Democrat, wasted little time in accusing the president of adding to the divisions that put an unwanted spotlight on the normally peaceful college town.

"Neo-Nazis, Klansmen and white supremacists came to Charlottesville heavily armed, spewing hatred and looking for a fight," Mr. McAuliffe said. "One of them murdered a young woman in an act of domestic terrorism, and two of our finest officers were killed in a tragic accident while serving to protect this community. This was not 'both sides.' "

No word in the Trump lexicon is as tread-worn as "unprecedented." But members of the president's staff, stunned and disheartened, said they never expected to hear such a voluble articulation of opinions that the president had long expressed in private. The National Economic Council chairman, Gary D. Cohn, and the Treasury secretary, Steven Mnuchin, who are Jewish, stood by uncomfortably as the president exacerbated a controversy that has once again engulfed a White House in disarray.

"I've condemned neo-Nazis," Mr. Trump told reporters, who interrupted him repeatedly when he seemed to equate the actions of protesters on each side.

He spoke of "very fine people on both sides." And of the demonstrators who rallied on Friday night, some chanting racist and anti-Semitic slogans, he said, "You had a lot of people in that group that were there to innocently protest and very legally protest."

Since the 1960s, Republican politicians have made muscular appeals to white voters, especially those in the South, on broad cultural grounds. But as a rule, they have taken a hard line on the party's racist, nativist and anti-Semitic fringe. Presidents Ronald Reagan, George Bush and George W. Bush roundly condemned white supremacists.

In 1991, President George Bush took on Mr. Duke, who was then seeking the governor's seat in Louisiana, saying, "When someone has so recently endorsed Nazism, it is inconceivable that someone can reasonably aspire to a leadership role in a free society."

But Mr. Trump, who has repeatedly said he is not prejudiced, has been equivocal in his public or private statements against white nationalists and other racist organizations.

On Saturday, in his first comments on Charlottesville, Mr. Trump blamed the violence on protesters from "many sides."

After a storm of criticism over his remarks, Mr. Trump's aides persuaded him to moderate his message by assigning explicit blame for the violence to far-right agitators, which led to a stronger denunciation of hate groups — emailed to reporters and attributed to an unnamed "spokesperson."

When that failed to quell the controversy, aides, including Mr. Trump's new chief of staff, John F. Kelly, pressed him to make another public statement. Mr. Trump's daughter Ivanka and son-in-law, Jared Kushner, urged him to take a more moderate stance, according to two people familiar with the situation. But as with so many other critical moments in Mr. Trump's presidency, the two were on vacation, this time in Vermont.

Grudgingly, Mr. Trump agreed.

"Racism is evil," the president said on Monday, delivering a statement from the White House that was written with aides during airplane and helicopter flights.

"Those who cause violence in its name are criminals and thugs, including the K.K.K., white supremacists and other hate groups," he added — in response to bipartisan condemnation of his more equivocal statements during the first 48 hours of the crisis.

But his unifying tone, which his staff characterized as more traditionally presidential, quickly gave way to a more familiar Trump approach. No sooner had he delivered the Monday statement than he began railing privately to his staff about the news media. He fumed to aides about how unfairly he was being treated, and expressed sympathy with nonviolent protesters who he said were defending their "heritage," according to a West Wing official.

He felt he had already given too much ground to his opponents, the official said.

Mr. Trump prides himself on an unapologetic style he learned from his father, Fred Trump, a New York City housing developer, and Roy Cohn, a combative lawyer who served as an aide to Senator Joseph McCarthy in the 1950s. During the 2016 presidential campaign, Mr. Trump attracted a significant following of white supremacists, expressed sympathy with white Southerners fighting to preserve monuments for Confederate icons and was slow to distance himself from racists like Mr. Duke.

The president's fury grew Monday as members of a White House business council began to resign to protest his reaction to Charlottesville. As usual, Mr. Trump found his voice by tweeting angrily about the news media.

By Tuesday afternoon, Mr. Trump's staff sensed the culmination of a familiar cycle: The president was about to revert to his initial, more defiant stance. As Mr. Trump approached the microphone in the lobby of Trump Tower on Tuesday, aides winced at the prospect of an unmediated president. With good reason.

"Alt-left" groups were also "very, very violent," Mr. Trump said early in his exchange with reporters.

He went on to assign "blame on both sides" — echoing his comments on Saturday, and reigniting a fight that has sunk staff morale after a brief bump in enthusiasm that followed the hiring of Mr. Kelly, who was to impose discipline on a chaotic West Wing.

Eric Cantor, a former Republican congressman from Virginia who was a member of Republican leadership, was horrified by what took place in Charlottesville, and said the president needed to have spoken out earlier.

"It really did demand a statement at the very beginning," said Mr. Cantor, who is Jewish. He added that efforts by the president to equate the actions of the counterprotesters, however violent they may have been, with the neo-Nazis and the driver of the car that murdered a protester were "unacceptable."

"There's no moral equivalence," Mr. Cantor said.

GLENN THRUSH reported from Washington, and **MAGGIE HABERMAN** from New York.

The State of the (White Nationalist) Union

OPINION | BY KASHANA CAULEY | JAN. 31, 2018

BEFORE LAST NIGHT'S State of the Union address, President Donald Trump invited news correspondents to the White House, where he told them, "I would like to see the country united." But hours later, he gave a speech meant to rally only part of the country.

He complimented coal and welding in a love letter to the white working classes of Appalachia and the Midwest. By admonishing people who don't stand for the national anthem, he reminded us that as president, he has picked fights with black N.F.L. players protesting police brutality. He repeatedly disparaged nonwhite people during his speech.

Instead of unifying the country, President Trump made it clear, yet again, that he supports only white Americans — to hell with everyone else.

The contrast between President Trump and President Barack Obama couldn't be more apparent. President Obama understood that our country's diversity was one of its greatest strengths and painted an inclusive picture of how America could move forward. "Our unique strengths as a nation — our optimism and work ethic, our spirit of discovery and innovation, our diversity and commitment to the rule of law," he said in 2016, in his last State of the Union address. "These things give us everything we need to ensure prosperity and security for generations to come."

But President Trump wants to divide the country between the white Americans he prizes and their purported foes, who may lurk around any corner unless he and Congress carry out the policies he described last night: the most extreme crackdown on immigration since 1924, an expansion of our nuclear arms program, the removal of federal employees who "undermine the public trust or fail the American people" and the continued operation of the military prison at Guantánamo Bay, which as of December 2017 held 41 people who are subject to indefinite detention in violation of due process.

This agenda is simply fear as national policy. What else explains Mr. Trump's talk about North Korea and nuclear weapons? Purging federal employees, while it may satisfy the president's need to punish his enemies, would mean, given his hiring record, that there would be fewer people in place to uphold our laws and carry out policies that help millions of Americans. The historic lows in African-American and Latino unemployment that he mentioned last night are partly a direct result of the productivity of hundreds of thousands of workers he wishes to deport.

President Trump made tokens of his minority guests, which underscored the point that he doesn't quite consider nonwhite people to be on a par with white Americans. Corey Adams, a black welder, was brought out as cover for the tax cut his employers at Staub Manufacturing Solutions in Dayton, Ohio, received under the Republicans' tax plan. Mr. Adams was in fact a reminder that working-class black people could reap minuscule benefits from tax cuts that will largely make the rich richer. But that's not all: President Trump also needed to tell us that Mr. Adams was an "all-American worker" to assure his xenophobic base that Mr. Adams couldn't possibly hail from somewhere else.

President Trump also introduced us to Celestino Martinez, an Immigration and Customs Enforcement agent who led an operation on Long Island to track down gang members, including members of MS-13. Mr. Trump introduced Mr. Martinez right after saying, "Americans are dreamers, too," to insult recipients of Deferred Action for Childhood Arrivals and illustrate that his American dream, instead of meaning the freedom to seek refuge on our shores and work toward a satisfying future, is based on arresting gang members. To make a Latino the face of ICE is a wink to Mr. Trump's base. It also says that Latinos can be trusted to follow the Trump agenda and throw people who look like them out of the country if they need to.

The most egregious case of tokenism was that of Evelyn Rodriguez and Freddy Cuevas, a couple whose daughter, Kayla Cuevas, was killed by MS-13 gang members on Long Island in 2016. Three days ago, Ms. Rodriguez said in an interview that she was happy to be invited to attend the State of the Union address but that her attendance wasn't about immigration. "I want him to ensure that we're going to get the proper funding for the resources for our kids," she said. "I'm not here for anyone's political gain." She added, "Everyone has the right to the American dream, and that should be there for them."

President Trump ignored Ms. Rodriguez's wishes. He pointed the couple out, claimed that bad immigration policy allowed the members of MS-13 who killed their daughter to come into the country and asked Congress to close "deadly" immigration loopholes that he blamed for her death. He used Ms. Rodriguez's pain to call for policies that she opposes.

President Trump's message is clear: Acceptable minorities work as ICE agents, help their employers take advantage of tax breaks and serve as visible reminders that people are killed by immigrants and foreigners.

This fatalist, white nationalist view of the world is a reminder that if last night was about unity, Mr. Trump cares to unite only white Americans.

KASHANA CAULEY is a television and freelance writer and a contributing opinion writer.

White Nationalists Love Corey Stewart. He Keeps Them Close.

BY DANNY HAKIM AND STEPHANIE SAUL | AUG. 5, 2018

The Republican nominee for Senate in Virginia likes to engage the racial fringes of his party, creating a dilemma for mainstream G.O.P. leaders wary of his views.

WOODBRIDGE, VA. — Corey Stewart stands at the end of a long driveway that leads back in time, to his 18th century plantation manor hidden in woods behind a modern housing development. Mr. Stewart, the Republican Senate nominee from Virginia, treats the brick home like a living museum, complete with buttons from Redcoats, a Civil War soldier's belt buckle and a room dedicated to George and Martha Washington, who were once visitors.

Both Mr. Stewart and his opponent, Senator Tim Kaine, were born in Minnesota, which makes it all the more unusual that Mr. Stewart has styled himself as a champion of the Confederacy and its statues, and, as he puts it, "taking back our heritage."

This has made him a popular figure with white nationalists, much to the horror of many Virginia Republicans. While Mr. Stewart has disavowed some on the extreme right, interviews with dozens of his friends, colleagues, supporters and fellow Republicans yielded a portrait of a political opportunist eager to engage the coarsest racial fringes of his party to advance his Trumpian appeal.

Some white nationalists volunteer for Mr. Stewart's campaign, and several of his aides and advisers have used racist or anti-Muslim language, or maintained links to outspoken racists like Jason Kessler, the organizer of last year's violent rally in Charlottesville, Va. Mr. Stewart has not distanced himself from those aides.

For mainstream Republicans in Virginia and nationwide, a profound political dilemma of the Trump era is whether to support the growing number of candidates like Mr. Stewart who make racially

STEPHEN VOSS FOR THE NEW YORK TIMES

Corey Stewart, the Republican nominee for Senate in Virginia, has styled himself as a champion of the Confederacy and its statues.

divisive remarks — particularly about immigrants — and back causes that are championed by white nationalists. President Trump's own language and policies have energized Mr. Stewart and other far-right candidates, and Mr. Trump has high approval ratings from Republicans, but it is not clear how many rank-and-file voters will embrace like-minded politicians like Mr. Stewart.

Mr. Trump has enthusiastically endorsed Mr. Stewart — tweeting in June: "Don't underestimate Corey, a major chance of winning!" — and the candidate is comfortable defending the president's most controversial comments. Sitting in the living room of the historic brick home he bought in 2012, Mr. Stewart praised President Trump's statement that there were "very fine people on both sides" at the Unite the Right white nationalist protests in Charlottesville last August.

"I don't think he said anything bad there," Mr. Stewart, 50, said during a 90-minute interview last month. "In fact I was one of the few people in the country that actually said pretty much the same thing."

He does not accept that slavery was at the heart of the Civil War.

"We can debate about the causes of the Civil War," he said, adding, "But the causes of it were much more complex" than only slavery.

"The question of what actually caused the Civil War is secondary to the result of the Civil War, which is that after the war was over, slavery was ended and the North and the South reconciled. And I think we need to respect that."

He contended that the term "white supremacist" was a concoction of the left.

"This term they literally resurrected, 'white supremacist,' which hadn't been used in 100 years, or whatever it was," he said, adding that "there's clearly a coordinated effort to — because they know the term 'racist' has been overused — they've come up with another one which is 'white supremacist,' an equally ridiculous term."

"I don't have a racist bone in my body," Mr. Stewart said during a recent appearance. "Not one. I challenge anybody to find a single racist statement that I've ever made."

In an extraordinary sign of discomfort with Mr. Stewart, some Republicans have been eager behind the scenes to provide opposition research aimed at discrediting him, with disaffected party members circulating racially inflammatory tweets and Facebook postings authored by one of Mr. Stewart's advisers.

Shaun Kenney, former state party executive director, lamented that "the alt-right has taken over the Virginia Republican Party." After Mr. Stewart secured the nomination in June, John C. Whitbeck, Jr., the party chairman who once accused Mr. Stewart of "racist" language, resigned.

But many Republican leaders haven't publicly disavowed Mr. Stewart, mindful that Mr. Trump is supporting him, and that the president has strong influence with the party base — many of whom supported Mr. Stewart in the primary.

Virginia has not elected a Republican statewide since 2009 and voted for Hillary Clinton over Mr. Trump in 2016. With its strong economy and elite public university system, Virginia has become a symbol of Southern moderation and tolerance, but the far right sees an ally in Mr. Stewart who will push back against the leftward drift and demographic changes underway in the state.

For his part, Mr. Stewart said he sees virtue in being provocative.

"I think you need to be edgy," he said.

"Controversy is not necessarily a bad thing, because it does give you more media attention and that's necessary, especially when you're in a position like mine," said Mr. Stewart, who is running well behind Mr. Kaine in the polls as well as fundraising. "I can't self-finance my race. And I don't have the support of the establishment. So I have to be my own guy."

'I WANTED MORE'

Even as a teenager growing up in Duluth, Mr. Stewart was known for his ambition.

"I had many kinds of debaters," his high school debate coach, Jack

JASON LAPPA FOR THE NEW YORK TIMES

Mr. Stewart, whose candidacy has the support of President Trump, said he sees virtue in being provocative.

Armstrong said. “Corey was a street smart debater,” he said, adding, “by the time he was a senior he was ranking with some of the best in the state.”

He came from a family of Democrats. His father was a longshoreman who couldn’t vote because of a felony conviction, Mr. Stewart said, adding it was “probably manslaughter” stemming from a fatal car accident. The younger Mr. Stewart was the first in his family to graduate from college, initially attending St. Olaf College in Minnesota, then transferring to Georgetown.

“I wanted more,” he said. “Nothing wrong with it, but I just wanted to see more.”

He eventually became an international trade lawyer and moved to Virginia, working at Foley & Lardner, a prominent firm. In 2006 he was elected chairman of the Prince William County Board, a county outside Washington, D.C., that has become majority minority in recent years.

In his politics, Mr. Stewart embraced expediency over ideology. He was initially anti-development, riding concerns about the pace of growth, then later allied with developers. Amid the county’s shifting demographics — its Hispanic population tripled rapidly — he picked up on immigration as a hot button. “I changed my focus to address what people were telling me their concerns were,” he said. “That’s how you get elected.”

Prince William County began questioning arrestees about their immigration status, then turning them over to federal agents.

Frank Principi, a Democrat on the board, said the county began to “detain people who did not look like us — different skin, different clothes, different language” and became known as *Condado del Diablo*, the devil’s county.

Many found the ease with which Mr. Stewart adopted hard-line views unsettling, starting with colleagues at work.

“Some of the partners at the firm didn’t like that very much,” Mr. Stewart said of his immigration stance, adding, “it became uncomfortable.”

He left in 2009 and began doing international trade work largely on his own. He also refashioned himself as a booster of the Confederacy, especially in his unsuccessful 2017 race for governor. He has appeared at the Old South Ball, an antebellum-dress event in Danville, and likened his own political crusade to that of Confederate rebels.

"You've got this guy who is a transplant coming into Virginia trying to out-Southern folks who've been here for 400 years," said Brian Schoeneman, a Fairfax Republican and former legislative candidate.

Mr. Stewart was aware of, but brushed aside, Robert E. Lee's prophetic warning that Confederate monuments could "keep open the sores of war."

"The monuments weren't contentious until the left started taking them down," Mr. Stewart said, adding that "thankfully those efforts seem to have subsided."

He claimed that "the ones who were most vehement in terms of taking down the monuments were not African-Americans. They were white liberals."

But Kevin Chandler, president of the state's N.A.A.C.P., called Mr. Stewart "treasonous" for his embrace of the Confederate flag.

"It symbolizes hate. It symbolizes white supremacy," the Rev. Chandler said. "And something such as that should not be displayed openly in the public."

Over the years, Mr. Stewart became increasingly outspoken. He dismissed one Republican rival as a "cuckservative" and assailed David Hogg, the teen gun control activist, as "that punk" who has "been brainwashed." He became an ardent defender of Alabama's Roy Moore amid allegations of sexual misconduct with underage girls. "I think they all disappeared since, didn't they?" he said of Mr. Moore's accusers. (They have not.)

At a board meeting this summer, one that Mr. Stewart did not attend, several speakers blamed him after Klan fliers landed on local lawns.

"This isn't a coincidence that this happened in my neighborhood," said Maggie Hansford, a local teacher who has decided to run for a board seat. "Our chairman can't stop talking about the Confederate flag."

Mr. Stewart later issued a statement condemning the Klan.

THE COMPANY HE KEEPS

A "Corey Stewart for Senate" sign flanks the gravel driveway leading to George and Donna Randall's southern Virginia home.

An avowed secessionist, Mr. Randall is eager to explain himself, welcoming a visitor onto his porch.

"I'm a secessionist because the federal government is anti-Christian and we're different culturally," explained Mr. Randall, a retired heavy equipment operator whose forebears include Confederate veterans. "The government never surrendered, only the Army. We're still under Reconstruction."

Interviews with Mr. Randall and his twin brother Gregory helped explain Mr. Stewart's appeal to his die-hard supporters.

"I liked Corey because he's a Trump supporter," said Gregory Randall, who plays Stonewall Jackson in Civil War re-enactments, in an interview at his home in Fredericksburg. "He's for low taxes, he's a big second amendment rights guy, he's against MS-13 and all these illegal people coming here that are committing crimes."

George Randall and his wife Donna have helped organize "meet and greets" for Mr. Stewart. The 60-year-old brothers have been seen frequently with him and are known to provide volunteer security for Mr. Stewart at public events, a task they both confirmed, though Mr. Stewart denied it, saying "that was one of those crazy rumors."

Both brothers took part in the Unite the Right rally and also belong to the League of the South, a Southern nationalist organization that honors John Wilkes Booth "for his service to the South" and seeks to secure "a future for white children."

Gregory was asked about anti-Semitic chanting that took place at the rally.

"The only thing that I think I heard somebody say was that 'Jews will not replace us,' " said Mr. Randall. "Wow, is that killing somebody?"

"Come on, it's a chant," he added. "The left chants stupid stuff all the time."

Such associations have dogged Mr. Stewart. He called a Wisconsin Congressional candidate, Paul Nehlen, "one of my personal heroes," long after Mr. Nehlen suggested American Muslims should be deported. Anti-Semitic rants finally prompted Mr. Stewart to disavow Mr. Nehlen.

"There's a guy that everybody supported before we all found out that he was a lunatic," Mr. Stewart said. "And many people said very kind things about him, even President Trump and Ann Coulter and Sarah Palin and Laura Ingraham."

But there are other ties. Mr. Stewart's press secretary also worked on Mr. Nehlen's campaign. Through a political action committee, so has his media adviser, Rick Shaftan, who is himself known for racially disparaging postings on social media. In an email, Mr. Shaftan called questions about his past remarks on race "absurd."

Mr. Stewart's associations with Mr. Kessler, the Charlottesville rally organizer, and Mr. Kessler's ties to a Stewart aide, Brian Landrum, have raised the most serious questions.

In February 2017, during his governor's race, Mr. Stewart appeared at a news conference with Mr. Kessler to oppose the Charlottesville City Council's decision to remove a Robert E. Lee statue from a park.

By then, Mr. Kessler's website included views associated with the so-called alt-right, a racist, far-right movement. During the news conference, Mr. Stewart said he had "nothing to do with that," but accompanied Mr. Kessler to deliver a court petition. Mr. Kessler also participated in a Charlottesville rally in support of the Lee statue sponsored by Mr. Stewart, and was alongside him at another event, where Mr. Stewart says Mr. Kessler "just happened to show up."

Mr. Stewart backed away from Mr. Kessler before Unite the Right last August. But afterward, in a Facebook video, he questioned why left-wing protesters shouldn't share equal blame.

One of Mr. Stewart's paid county staff members — Mr. Landrum — has maintained ties with Mr. Kessler, according to court documents. Mr. Landrum recently took part in a Facebook chat with about 20 people, including violent racists, planning a second Unite the Right rally later this month.

Mr. Landrum, who also worked in Mr. Stewart's campaigns, commented only once on the chat, on May 17, with smiley emojis and profanity.

In a July deposition in a dispute with the city over a proposed rally this month in Charlottesville, Mr. Kessler described Mr. Landrum as a friend. "Have you had discussions with him in the last couple months?" Mr. Kessler was asked. "Yes," he answered.

Mr. Stewart declined to comment, referring questions to Mr. Landrum, who did not return messages seeking comment. An attempt to reach him at his Woodbridge, Va., apartment resulted in a police complaint that a reporter for The New York Times entered his dwelling unlawfully, an allegation The Times has denied.

Mr. Stewart brushed off questions about the company he keeps, and returned repeatedly in the interview to his love of his adopted state's heritage, and his admiration for the president.

"All these attacks, on all this Kessler stuff and everything else like that, most people are just, they don't believe it," he said. "They are so used to the left calling Trump and other conservatives as racists and bigots."

"I'm not going to back down from my controversial positions," he added. "If I were to do that my base would be gone. And so my strategy is just, continue to speak the truth, even if it is controversial."

JACK BEGG, **DORIS BURKE** and **ALAIN DELAQUÉRIÈRE** contributed research.

Trump's Potent Toxicity

OPINION | BY CHARLES M. BLOW | OCT. 28, 2018

Trump has flirted with the deepest racists and Nazis and it has not gone unnoticed, least of all by them.

OUR NATIONAL DIALOGUE about diversity and inclusion, about acceptance and egalitarianism, is poisoned, and Donald Trump is holding a rather large pouch of poison.

Last week, we saw the arrest of a Trump supporter who sent pipe bombs through the mail to people who were frequent rhetorical targets of the president, many of them prominent Democrats, including former President Barack Obama.

Then on Saturday came a mass shooting at a Jewish synagogue by a rabid anti-Semite. As NBC reported:

"The shooting at the Tree of Life Synagogue in Pittsburgh — in which the death toll now stands at 11 — is believed to be the deadliest attack on the Jewish community in the history of the U.S., the Anti-Defamation League said."

According to CNN, the shooter, Robert Bowers, was a man who claimed on the social media app Gab, a nest of white nationalists and the 'alt-right,' that Jews were behind the migrant caravans. NBC News put it this way:

"Bowers frequently posted about the 'migrant caravan,' a group of several thousand refugees walking to the U.S.-Mexico border from Honduras to seek asylum. Preventing refugees in the caravan from entering the U.S. has been a major talking point among both right-wing commentators and President Donald Trump, who has spoken about it in recent pre-midterm election stump speeches."

There is no way to separate Trump from the fulminating against the caravans.

And yet, even Trump appears to have been too mild a racist and "nationalist" for the synagogue shooter. As CNN notes, "roughly four hours before the shooting, Bowers commented in a post that he did not vote for Trump." He once posted "Trump is a globalist, not a nationalist," and he has posted that Trump is surrounded by too many Jewish people.

Therein lies the uneasy alliance: The white nationalists, neo-Nazis and alt-right are energized by Trump's election, and yet many find his white power positioning falls short of their own.

That doesn't mean that Trump doesn't court their support and defend their actions.

After the alt-right staged its deadly march in Charlottesville, in which throngs of marchers with torches chanted "Jews will not replace us," Trump insisted that there had been "very fine people on both sides" of the protest.

When Richard Spencer, a white nationalist who helped organize the Charlottesville rally, spoke to reporters last year, Business Insider reported:

"Asked whether he considers Trump an ally, Spencer replied that while he didn't think of Trump as 'alt-right,' he considers the president to be 'the first true authentic nationalist in my lifetime.' "

As The Atlantic has reported, Spencer "gained international notoriety just after the 2016 election for giving a speech in Washington, D.C., in which he declared 'Hail Trump!,' prompting Nazi salutes from his audience."

In an interview with Vice, Christopher Cantwell, who was also involved in the Charlottesville march, had this exchange with the interviewer over the issue of white violence:

Cantwell: "I'm here to spread ideas, talk in the hopes that somebody more capable will come along and do that, somebody like Donald Trump who does not give his daughter to a Jew."

Interviewer: "So Donald Trump, but like, more racist?"

Cantwell: "A lot more racist than Donald Trump. I don't think that you could feel about race the way I do and watch that Kushner bastard walk around with that beautiful girl."

That of course was a reference to Ivanka Trump's husband, Jared Kushner.

So these folks are emboldened by Trump, but now that they have an inch, they want a mile. Still there is clearly something happening on the ground that is undeniable. As The New York Times reported on Saturday:

"According to an annual report by the Anti-Defamation League issued earlier this year, the number of reported anti-Semitic incidents in the United States surged 57 percent in 2017, the largest rise in a single year since the A.D.L. began tracking such crimes in 1979."

2017, of course, was the first year of the Trump administration.

As always, this cautionary note must be included: Homicidal maniacs are responsible for their own actions. It is almost impossible in most cases to attach the words of one person to the deeds of another.

However, it must also be said that Trump has produced a toxic environment of intolerance in this country that is deep and wide. He has flirted with the deepest racists and Nazis and it has not gone unnoticed, least of all by them.

Last week at a debate, Florida's Democratic gubernatorial hopeful Andrew Gillum said of his Republican opponent, Ron DeSantis: "I'm not calling Mr. DeSantis a racist, I'm simply saying the racists believe he's a racist."

I believe that the same could be said of Trump, although he engages in his own strain of racism.

CHARLES BLOW joined The Times in 1994 and became an Opinion columnist in 2008. He is also a television commentator and writes often about politics, social justice and vulnerable communities.

Standing 'Against White Supremacy,' G.O.P. Campaign Chief Rebukes Steve King

BY CATIE EDMONDSON | OCT. 30, 2018

WASHINGTON — As Pittsburgh began burying the victims of Saturday's synagogue massacre, the head of the House Republican campaign arm all but jettisoned Representative Steve King of Iowa from the House Republican Conference, declaring, "We must stand up against white supremacy and hate in all forms."

The highly unusual rebuke by Representative Steve Stivers of Ohio, the chairman of the National Republican Congressional Committee, came a week before the midterm elections — but after years of incendiary and racially charged comments by Mr. King, capped in recent days by his endorsement of a white nationalist running for mayor of Toronto and a meeting with Austrian white nationalists, which he funded through a trip to visit concentration camps.

Mr. King is also locked in the toughest re-election fight of his eight-term House career.

"Congressman Steve King's recent comments, actions, and retweets are completely inappropriate," Mr. Stivers wrote on Twitter. "We must stand up against white supremacy and hate in all forms, and I strongly condemn this behavior."

Mr. King fired back with a statement of his own, affirming that Americans of all races and "national origins-legal immigrants & natural born citizens" are created equal. He blamed attacks on him as "orchestrated by nasty, desperate, and dishonest fake news," aided by complicit "Establishment Never Trumpers."

The public censure is the latest downturn for Mr. King, whose lengthy history of making racially charged remarks has been subjected to closer scrutiny after the synagogue shooting in Pittsburgh.

After liberal activists on social media lobbied some of Mr. King's corporate donors to cut ties with the representative, the Midwestern dairy giant Land O'Lakes withdrew its support, saying in a statement that it wants its "contributions to be a positive force for good."

New polling from Iowa's Fourth Congressional District indicates that he is in a statistical tie with his Democratic opponent, J. D. Scholten, a former baseball player and a first-time candidate, who has significantly outraised him. Iowa Republicans are already at risk of losing two other House seats.

Over nearly 16 years, Mr. King has evolved from a stalwart conservative to a vocal opponent of immigration to the edge of white supremacy. He compared immigrants to dogs and said young migrants had "calves the size of cantaloupes" because they were hauling in bales of marijuana. He once tweeted a political cartoon depicting President Barack Obama wearing a turban.

Two weeks ago, he endorsed Faith Goldy, who has previously recited the 14-word manifesto used by neo-Nazis, in her race for Toronto mayor. And in the spring, he retweeted an anti-immigration message from a prominent Nazi sympathizer who has described himself as an admirer of Hitler. (Mr. King defended that decision, adding, "I will retweet the devil if the devil tweets, 'I Love Jesus.' It's the message, not the messenger.")

But the tipping point may have come last week when news reports revealed that Mr. King had met in August with members of an Austrian political party associated with neo-Nazi movements while he was on a trip to Holocaust sites that was funded by a Holocaust memorial charity, From the Depths.

His local newspaper, The Sioux City Journal, which had endorsed Mr. King in previous races, instead endorsed Mr. Scholten.

"Each time King immerses himself in controversy, he holds up this district to ridicule and marginalizes himself within the legislative body he serves," the newspaper's editorial board wrote, "neither of which provides benefit to Iowans who live and work here."

Far-Right Internet Groups Listen for Trump's Approval, and Often Hear It

BY KEVIN ROOSE AND ALI WINSTON | NOV. 4, 2018

ON WEDNESDAY, MINUTES AFTER President Trump posted an incendiary campaign ad falsely accusing Democrats of flooding the country with murderous illegal immigrants, virulent racists on an online message board erupted in celebration.

"I love it. We should be making videos like this," one said. Another approvingly compared the ad to "With Open Gates," a viral 2015 video about the dangers of European immigration that drew praise from prominent neo-Nazis and white nationalists, and was broadly condemned by anti-hate groups.

These posts, which appeared on the politics forum of 4chan, an online message board known for hosting extreme speech and graphic imagery, were not a one-off. In recent weeks, as Mr. Trump and his allies have waged a fear-based campaign to drive Republican voters to the polls for the midterm elections on Tuesday, far-right internet communities have been buoyed as their once-fringe views have been given oxygen by prominent Republicans.

These activists cheered when Mr. Trump suggested that the Jewish billionaire George Soros could be secretly funding a caravan of Latin American migrants — a dog-whistle reference to an anti-Semitic conspiracy theory that has been advanced by neo-Nazis and white nationalists for years. They roared their approval when Mr. Trump began stirring up fears of angry, violent left-wing mobs, another far-right boogeyman. And they have found traces of their ideas in Mr. Trump's rhetoric, including his concern for an obscure land rights conflict involving white farmers in South Africa and his references to asylum-seeking migrants as "invaders."

"Most of these conspiracies are not new to us," said Oren Segal, the director of the Anti-Defamation League's Center on Extremism. "I've seen white supremacists and extremists talk about these anti-Semitic and racist ideas for years. But it was always in the corner. Now, you don't know where the mainstream starts and the fringe ends."

Since the 2016 election, these far-right communities have entered into a sort of imagined dialogue with the president. They create and disseminate slogans and graphics, and celebrate when they show up in Mr. Trump's Twitter feed days or weeks later. They carefully dissect his statements, looking for hints of their influence. And when they find those clues, they take them as evidence that Mr. Trump is "/ourguy/," a label for people internet extremists believe share their views, but who are unable to say so directly in public.

"There's this feedback loop between Donald Trump's Twitter feed and right-wing extremist movements," said Sophie Bjork-James, an assistant professor of anthropology at Vanderbilt University who has studied far-right extremism. "They're not all supportive of Trump, but his language does give them ideas that then circulate online in extremist social media spaces."

The White House press office did not respond to multiple requests for comment.

Right-wing extremists — a catchall category for a messy constellation of neo-Nazis, white nationalists, crypto-fascists, nihilists and attention-seeking trolls — vary widely in style and ideology. Some congregate out in the open, on forums like 4chan and Reddit as well as public platforms like Gab, the Twitter-like social network used by the suspect in the Pittsburgh synagogue shooting. Others communicate in private channels on Discord, a chat platform, or over encrypted messaging apps like Telegram or Wire. Some are ardent supporters of Mr. Trump, while others oppose him on the grounds that he is not extreme enough.

What they have in common is a feeling of empowerment — a sense that the boundaries of acceptable speech are widening in the Trump era, and a suspicion that when they talk, Mr. Trump, or those with access to him, may be listening.

DOUG MILLS/THE NEW YORK TIMES

As President Trump and his allies have waged a fear-based campaign to drive Republican voters to the polls, far-right communities have parsed his statements, looking for hints of their influence.

Even small phrases can set off speculation. Last month, when Mr. Trump tweeted an unfounded accusation that left-wing protesters outside the confirmation hearings for Justice Brett M. Kavanaugh were "paid for by Soros and others," some extremists took it as evidence that the president shared their view of a global Jewish-led conspiracy led by Mr. Soros, a leading donor to many liberal causes.

"Trump has officially named the Jew," wrote one user on 4chan. "Trump knows," wrote another, who said that the "others" Mr. Trump referred to in his tweet might be a sly reference to other shadowy Jewish benefactors.

These extremists' sense of influence is almost certainly exaggerated. Mr. Trump, who has Jewish family members including his daughter, has said nothing about Mr. Soros's religion or a larger Jewish conspiracy. And it is unlikely that the president, who has said that he does not use a computer, is wading through obscure message boards in search of talking points.

But that hasn't stopped those extremists from interpreting his words as a signal that the president shares their views.

It is difficult to quantify how many right-wing extremists exist in America — many operate anonymously or pseudonymously online, and few real-world gatherings take place. But some private channels for neo-Nazis and other extremist groups have thousands of members, and more mainstream right-wing spaces — such as a pro-Trump Reddit forum, r/the_donald, which has more than 600,000 members — have amplified extremist messages.

Last month, users on r/the_donald promoted a slogan — "jobs, not mobs." They said the phrase, which has historical roots in right-wing fears of violence by anti-fascist protest groups, would make a good closing argument for Republicans in this year's midterm elections.

"Jobs not mobs" appears to have taken off with help from Scott Adams, the "Dilbert" cartoonist and a self-styled communications guru who is popular with the pro-Trump internet crowd. Mr. Adams said on Twitter that the phrase was likely to be persuasive to voters because it rhymed, and that it was "brain glue plus framing and contrast."

The slogan was then turned into an image meme — a split-screen photo showing busy factory workers in contrast with angry protesters — and posted to the r/the_donald forum, where it drew rave reviews from thousands of members. From there, it spread to prominent conservative commentators on Twitter and Fox News, who used it to stir fears of left-wing mob violence. And on Oct. 18, six days after #jobsnotmobs appeared on a right-wing Reddit forum, Mr. Trump tweeted it.

Since then, the phrase has become a Republican mantra. It has featured prominently in campaign ads, has been grafted onto T-shirts and legions of internet images, and has been chanted by crowds at rallies for Republican candidates.

Mr. Trump may not be consciously egging on these efforts. But experts in online extremism say that his reluctance to rein in the radical elements of his base — perhaps best expressed by his kid-gloves treatment of white nationalists after the deadly "Unite the Right" rally in Charlottesville, Va., last year — have created an opening for more extreme ideas to spread.

Joan Donovan, a researcher at the think tank Data & Society who studies right-wing extremism online, said the far right corners of the internet often serve as an ad hoc testing ground for political messages that move fringe ideas into the mainstream.

"They incubate online, in YouTube videos, articles, through influencers, and they slowly become divorced from their politicized roots," Ms. Donovan said.

Ms. Donovan cited the example of Lauren Southern, a far-right YouTube personality who led a successful campaign to gain mainstream traction with an exaggerated story about land being seized from white farmers in South Africa. The story, a long-running narrative among white nationalists, has been used to further racist fears of an impending "white genocide" at the hands of black South Africans.

Ms. Southern campaigned to place the story in right-wing media in the United States, making personal appeals to top conservative media figures. Eventually, Tucker Carlson, the Fox News commentator, covered the story in a segment, and Mr. Trump tweeted about the issue, mentioning Mr. Carlson and Fox News in the tweet.

The president's surfacing of the white farmer issue did not escape the notice of the far right. On an episode this year of White Rabbit Radio, a podcast that promotes extremist views, an anonymous commentator said that Mr. Trump's remarks had legitimized a decades-old, obscure issue for white nationalists.

"This was the province of Stormfront five, 10 years ago," the commenter said, referring to a neo-Nazi internet forum. "Now, it is mainstream."

The ability of online extremists to push, tailor and amplify political messages has turned them into a potent force in the age of internet politics, as candidates and elected officials look to what is popular online to shape their own messages.

"I don't think Trump is setting the agenda here," Ms. Donovan said. "He's riding a wave of attention that is primarily being played out and happening online. He wouldn't have the ability to launch these policies if there wasn't a quorum of people online getting ready to back him up and push these ideas across multiple platforms."

Even when Mr. Trump denounces extremism, many of his supporters online see it as a begrudging concession, rather than an expression of his true beliefs. Last weekend, as Mr. Trump spoke about the dangers of anti-Semitism in the wake of the mass shooting at the Tree of Life synagogue in Pittsburgh, internet bigots reassured each other that Mr. Trump was still on their side.

"He needs to spin this for the midterms," one poster on 4chan wrote.

"He really is playing 5D chess," wrote another.

Not every online activist has the goal of shaping Mr. Trump's thinking on hot-button issues, of course. For some, just being noticed is the prize.

After Mr. Trump tweeted the "jobs, not mobs" meme, the creator of the image — a Reddit user who goes by the online pen name "Bryan Machiavelli" and who declined to be interviewed unless The New York Times paid him $200 an hour for his "memetic warfare consulting" services — wrote on Reddit that attention from the president was its own reward.

"I am so excited that I achieved a goal I set 2 years ago," he wrote, "to have the president retweet a meme I made."

CHAPTER 5

Charlottesville

In August 2017, white nationalist groups organized a "Unite the Right" rally that took place in Charlottesville, Va. What followed were several days of protests and violence as white nationalists clashed with leftist demonstrators. The conflict culminated in one white nationalist driving a car through a crowd of people, taking a young woman's life. The articles in this section include reporting from that day as well as its aftermath.

White Nationalists March on University of Virginia

BY HAWES SPENCER AND SHERYL GAY STOLBERG | AUG. 11, 2017

CHARLOTTESVILLE, VA. — A month after a Ku Klux Klan rally here ended with the police using tear gas on protesters, Charlottesville is bracing for a weekend of white nationalist demonstrations and counterprotests, and suddenly this tranquil college town feels like a city under siege.

Thousands of people — many from out of town — are expected to descend on the city to either protest or participate in a "Unite the Right" rally on Saturday convened by white nationalists who oppose a plan to remove a statue of Robert E. Lee, the Confederate general, from a city park.

"People are angry, they're scared, they're hurt, they're confused," said the Rev. Seth Wispelwey of the local United Church of Christ. "White supremacists rallying in our town is an act of violence."

Late Friday night, several hundred torch-bearing men and women marched on the main quadrangle of the University of Virginia's grounds, shouting, "You will not replace us," and "Jew will not replace us." They walked around the Rotunda, the university's signature building, and to a statue of Thomas Jefferson, where a group of counterprotesters were gathered, and a brawl ensued. At least one person was led away in handcuffs by the police.

In a Facebook post, Charlottesville's mayor, Mike Signer, called it a "cowardly parade of hatred, bigotry, racism, and intolerance."

"I am beyond disgusted by this unsanctioned and despicable display of visual intimidation on a college campus," he added.

City officials and the police said they were prepared for possible unrest; the Virginia National Guard put out a statement saying it would "closely monitor the situation." Mayor Mike Signer said in an interview on Friday that he had been consulting with fellow mayors, seeking advice on how to "be prepared to make sure people can assemble and express themselves freely."

Religious leaders who are planning counterdemonstrations — including a sunrise prayer service featuring Cornel West, the Harvard professor and political activist — have been training in nonviolent protest.

The University of Virginia Medical Center has canceled all elective surgery — standard procedure in preparation for events that could lead to mass casualties. Around town, some businesses plan to close.

"This whole thing feels like the prep to a Wild West shootout where the businesses shutter and the women shoo their children upstairs," said Phillip Fassieux, 36, as he munched on an egg bagel at Bodo's, a few blocks from the Lee statue. "This isn't the wild, wild West. This is modern-day Charlottesville, where we're supposed to be better suited to engage with each other."

With the university, founded by Jefferson in 1819, as its centerpiece, Charlottesville is a politically progressive city; nearly 80 percent of voters here cast their ballots for Hillary Clinton in last year's presidential race.

But it is also a city steeped in Southern history, one that still wrestles with the legacy of slavery. According to Jalane Schmidt, a professor of religious studies at the university, 52 percent of the residents of Charlottesville and surrounding Albemarle County — 14,000 people in all — were enslaved during the Civil War. Jefferson, still revered here, was himself a slave owner.

Today, African-Americans make up 19 percent of the city's population, and gentrification is pushing many of them out, Ms. Schmidt said. The fight over the Lee statue — in a downtown park that was called Lee Park until it was recently renamed Emancipation Park — has opened up old wounds and brought simmering tensions over race to the fore.

Eugene Williams, 89, a former head of the local N.A.A.C.P., served sweet tea on the front porch of his house on Ridge Street one day this week and recalled the days when he was not allowed to dine at local restaurants. He favors keeping the Lee statue because he wants people to remember the Jim Crow era.

"This statue has a lesson to teach us," he said.

The debate over the statue began about a year and a half ago, when an African-American high school student here started a petition to have it removed. Wes Bellamy, the city's vice mayor and the only black member of the City Council, took up the cause, and the Council set up a commission. After public hearings, it recommended either that the statue be relocated to another park or that the city add historical context so that the monument could "transform in place."

Instead, City Council members voted 3 to 2 in April to sell the statue. The next month, a judge issued an injunction, keeping the statue in place for six months.

"Charlottesville kind of made itself a target by deciding they wanted to remove this statue, and by stringing the whole thing out," said Douglas Laycock, a University of Virginia law professor who is planning to give a talk on free speech Saturday as part of a "day of reflective conversation" organized by the university.

Mr. Bellamy, 30, has himself become a target; he said in an interview that he has been receiving death threats. "When you have a black, young African-American vice mayor, in their eyes, who was getting too big for his breeches, they want to send a message," he said. "They call me every kind of N-word you can think of."

The conflict drew the attention of two white nationalists — Richard B. Spencer and Jason Kessler, both University of Virginia graduates. In May, Mr. Spencer, who gained national notoriety after the election of President Trump, led a gathering of torch-wielding protesters to the statue, which depicts Lee on horseback. At a Ku Klux Klan rally on July 8, the state police used pepper spray to disperse protesters, officials said.

Mr. Kessler, who organized the event on Saturday and calls himself a "white advocate," said in an interview that his goal was to "de-stigmatize white advocacy so that white people can stand up for their interests just like any other identity group."

In the run-up to Saturday, there has been confusion over where, precisely, the Unite the Right rally will take place. City officials denied Mr. Kessler's request to hold it in Emancipation Park, and instead granted a permit for a bigger park. On Thursday, the American Civil Liberties Union filed a lawsuit on behalf of Mr. Kessler, seeking to keep the demonstration at Emancipation Park.

On Friday, a judge ruled in Mr. Kessler's favor.

But if the city seems seized with anxiety, there is also a sense of determination.

"Charlottesville is mobilizing," said Mimi Arbeit, a community activist who is helping to organize counterdemonstrations. "We cannot allow the rise of white supremacy. Ignoring the Klan in the 1920s is precisely what allowed them to terrorize and murder black people in Charlottesville. We cannot allow that history to be repeated."

HAWES SPENCER reported from Charlottesville, and **SHERYL GAY STOLBERG** from Washington.

Man Charged After White Nationalist Rally in Charlottesville Ends in Deadly Violence

BY SHERYL GAY STOLBERG AND BRIAN M. ROSENTHAL | AUG. 12, 2017

CHARLOTTESVILLE, VA. — The city of Charlottesville was engulfed by violence on Saturday as white nationalists and counterprotesters clashed in one of the bloodiest fights to date over the removal of Confederate monuments across the South.

White nationalists had long planned a demonstration over the city's decision to remove a statue of Robert E. Lee. But the rally quickly exploded into racial taunting, shoving and outright brawling, prompting the governor to declare a state of emergency and the National Guard to join the police in clearing the area.

Those skirmishes mostly resulted in cuts and bruises. But after the rally at a city park was dispersed, a car bearing Ohio license plates plowed into a crowd near the city's downtown mall, killing a 32-year-old woman. Some 34 others were injured, at least 19 in the car crash, according to a spokeswoman for the University of Virginia Medical Center.

Col. Martin Kumer, the superintendent of the Albemarle-Charlottesville Regional Jail, confirmed Saturday evening that an Ohio man, James Alex Fields Jr., 20, of Maumee, had been arrested and charged with second-degree murder, three counts of malicious wounding and failing to stop at the scene of a crash that resulted in a death. But the authorities declined to say publicly that Mr. Fields was the driver of the car that plowed into the crowd.

Witnesses to the crash said a gray sports car accelerated into a crowd of counterdemonstrators — who were marching jubilantly near the mall after the white nationalists had left — and hurled at least two people in the air.

"It was probably the scariest thing I've ever seen in my life," said Robert Armengol, who was at the scene reporting for a podcast he hosts with students at the University of Virginia. "After that it was pandemonium. The car hit reverse and sped and everybody who was up the street in my direction started running."

The planned rally was promoted as "Unite the Right" and both its organizers and critics said they expected it to be one of the largest gatherings of white nationalists in recent times, attracting groups like the Ku Klux Klan and neo-Nazis and movement leaders like David Duke and Richard Spencer.

Many of these groups have felt emboldened since the election of Donald J. Trump as president. Mr. Duke, a former imperial wizard of the Ku Klux Klan, told reporters on Saturday that the protesters were "going to fulfill the promises of Donald Trump" to "take our country back."

Saturday afternoon, President Trump, speaking at the start of a veterans' event at his golf club in Bedminster, N.J., addressed what he described as "the terrible events unfolding in Charlottesville, Virginia."

In his comments, President Trump condemned the bloody protests, but he did not specifically criticize the white nationalist rally and its neo-Nazi slogans, blaming "hatred, bigotry and violence on many sides."

"It's been going on for a long time in our country, it's not Donald Trump, it's not Barack Obama," said Mr. Trump, adding that he had been in contact with Virginia officials. After calling for the "swift restoration of law and order," he offered a plea for unity among Americans of "all races, creeds and colors."

The president came under criticism from some who said he had not responded strongly enough against racism and that he failed to condemn the white nationalist groups by name who were behind the rally.

Among those displeased with Mr. Trump was the mayor of Charlottesville, Mike Signer. "I do hope that he looks himself in the mirror and thinks very deeply about who he consorted with during his campaign," he said.

Late on Saturday night, the Department of Justice announced that it was opening a civil rights investigation into "the circumstances of the deadly vehicular incident," to be conducted by the F.B.I., the United States attorney for the Western District of Virginia, and the department's Civil Rights Division.

"The violence and deaths in Charlottesville strike at the heart of American law and justice," Attorney General Jeff Sessions said in a statement. "When such actions arise from racial bigotry and hatred, they betray our core values and cannot be tolerated."

The turmoil in Charlottesville began with a march Friday night by white nationalists on the campus of the University of Virginia and escalated Saturday morning as demonstrators from both sides gathered in and around the park. Waving Confederate flags, chanting Nazi-era slogans, wearing helmets and carrying shields, the white nationalists converged on the Lee statue inside the park and began chanting phrases like "You will not replace us" and "Jews will not replace us."

Hundreds of counterprotesters — religious leaders, Black Lives Matter activists and anti-fascist groups known as "antifa" — quickly surrounded the park, singing spirituals, chanting and carrying their own signs.

The morning started peacefully, with the white nationalists gathering in McIntire Park, outside downtown, and the counterdemonstrators — including Cornel R. West, the Harvard University professor and political activist — gathering at the First Baptist Church, a historically African-American church here. Professor West, who addressed the group at a sunrise prayer service, said he had come "bearing witness to love and justice in the face of white supremacy."

At McIntire Park, the white nationalists waved Confederate flags and other banners. One of the participants, who gave his name only as Ted because he said he might want to run for political office some day, said he was from Missouri, and added, "I'm tired of seeing white people pushed around."

But by 11 a.m., after both sides had made their way to Emancipation Park, the scene had exploded into taunting, shoving and outright brawling. Three people were arrested in connection with the skirmishes.

Barricades encircling the park and separating the two sides began to come down, and the police temporarily retreated. People were seen clubbing one another in the streets, and pepper spray filled the air. One of the white nationalists left the park bleeding, his head wrapped in gauze.

Declaring the gathering an unlawful assembly, the police had cleared the area before noon, and the Virginia National Guard arrived as officers began arresting some who remained. But fears lingered that the altercation would start again nearby, as demonstrators dispersed in smaller groups.

Within an hour, politicians, including Gov. Terry McAuliffe, a Democrat, and the House speaker, Paul D. Ryan of Wisconsin, a Republican, had condemned the violence.

The first public response from the White House came from the first lady, Melania Trump, who wrote on Twitter: "Our country encourages freedom of speech, but let's communicate w/o hate in our hearts. No good comes from violence."

Former President Barack Obama responded to the violence on Twitter with a quote from Nelson Mandela: "No one is born hating another person because of the color of his skin or his background or his religion... People must learn to hate, and if they can learn to hate, they can be taught to love.."

After the rally was dispersed, its organizer, Jason Kessler, who calls himself a "white advocate," complained in an interview that his group had been "forced into a very chaotic situation." He added, "The police were supposed to be there protecting us and they stood down."

Both Mr. Kessler and Richard Spencer, a prominent white nationalist who was to speak on Saturday, are graduates of the University of Virginia. In an online video, titled "a message to Charlottesville," Mr. Spencer vowed to return to the college town.

"You think that we're going to back down to this kind of behavior to you and your little provincial town? No," he said. "We are going to make Charlottesville the center of the universe."

Later in the day, a Virginia State Police helicopter crashed near a golf course and burst into flames. The pilot, Lt. H. Jay Cullen, 48, of Midlothian, Va., and Berke M. M. Bates, 40, a trooper-pilot of Quinton, Va., died at the scene. Their Bell 407 helicopter was assisting with the situation in Charlottesville, the Virginia State Police said.

The violence in Charlottesville was the latest development in a series of tense dramas unfolding across the United States over plans to remove statues and other historical markers of the Confederacy. The battles have been intensified by the election of Mr. Trump, who enjoys fervent support from white nationalists.

In New Orleans, tempers flared this spring when four Confederate-era monuments were taken down. Hundreds of far-right and liberal protesters squared off, with occasional bouts of violence, under another statue of Robert E. Lee. There were fisticuffs and a lot of shouting, but nothing like the violence seen in Charlottesville.

In St. Louis, workers removed a confederate monument from Forest Park in June, ending a drawn-out battle over its fate. In Frederick, Md., a bust of Roger B. Taney, the chief justice of the United States who wrote the notorious 1857 Dred Scott decision denying blacks citizenship, was removed in May from its spot near City Hall.

Here in Charlottesville, Saturday's protest was the culmination of a year and a half of debate over the Lee statue. A movement to withdraw it began when an African-American high school student here started a petition. The City Council voted 3 to 2 in April to sell it, but a judge issued an injunction temporarily stopping the move.

The city had been bracing for a sea of demonstrators, and on Friday night, hundreds of them, carrying lit torches, marched on the picturesque grounds of the University of Virginia, founded in 1819 by Thomas Jefferson.

"We're going to fulfill the promises of Donald Trump" to "take our country back," said Mr. Duke, a former imperial wizard of the Ku Klux

Klan. Many of the white nationalist protesters carried campaign signs for Mr. Trump.

University officials said one person was arrested and charged Friday night with assault and disorderly conduct, and several others were injured. Among those hurt was a university police officer injured while making the arrest, the school said in a statement.

Teresa A. Sullivan, the president of the university, strongly condemned the Friday demonstration in a statement, calling it "disturbing and unacceptable."

Still, officials allowed the Saturday protest to go on — until the injuries began piling up.

Charlottesville declared a state of emergency around 11 a.m., citing an "imminent threat of civil disturbance, unrest, potential injury to persons, and destruction of public and personal property."

Governor McAuliffe followed with his own declaration an hour later.

"It is now clear that public safety cannot be safeguarded without additional powers, and that the mostly-out-of-state protesters have come to Virginia to endanger our citizens and property," he said in a statement. "I am disgusted by the hatred, bigotry and violence these protesters have brought to our state."

The Republican candidate for governor in Virginia, Ed Gillespie, issued his own statement denouncing the protests as "vile hate" that has "no place in our Commonwealth."

Mr. Ryan agreed. "The views fueling the spectacle in Charlottesville are repugnant," he said on Twitter. "Let it only serve to unite Americans against this kind of vile bigotry."

SHERYL GAY STOLBERG reported from Charlottesville, and **BRIAN M. ROSENTHAL** from New York. **HAWES SPENCER** contributed reporting from Charlottesville, and **CHARLIE SAVAGE** from Washington.

Far-Right Groups Surge Into National View in Charlottesville

BY RICHARD FAUSSET AND ALAN FEUER | AUG. 13, 2017

IT WAS A DEADLY weekend of rage-fueled street battles. And after the violent demonstrations in Charlottesville, Va., leaders of white nationalist groups claimed success.

"It was a huge moral victory in terms of the show of force," said Richard B. Spencer, the far-right figure who had come to Charlottesville to speak at Saturday morning's "Unite the Right" rally.

The declaration from Mr. Spencer, in an interview late Saturday, was typical of the man who has rhetorically elbowed his way into the national conversation with his use of Nazi language and his unalloyed contention that America belongs to white people.

And indeed, the demonstrations in Charlottesville were perhaps the most visible manifestation to date of the evolution of the American far right, a coalition of old and new white supremacist groups connected by social media and emboldened by the election of Donald J. Trump.

Yet it is by no means clear what the demonstrations mean for the future of this movement and what, if any, lasting effect they will have. Will the overt displays of racism return the extreme right-wing to the margins of politics, or will they serve to normalize the movement, allowing it to weave itself deeper into the national conversation?

Many Americans watched transfixed as members of those groups marched down the street, barked out anti-Semitic chants and openly displayed the symbols of Nazi Germany and the secessionist South.

And many looked on in horror as a speeding car crashed into other vehicles on a crowded street Saturday afternoon, resulting in the death of a 32-year-old woman and injuries to at least 19 other people.

Though President Trump, in his comments, declined to single out the white supremacist movement, many mainstream conservatives were appalled. Senator John McCain called the white supremacists "traitors" on Twitter.

The House speaker, Paul D. Ryan, called them "repugnant."

The Justice Department announced late Saturday that it was opening a civil rights investigation. "The violence and deaths in Charlottesville strike at the heart of American law and justice," Attorney General Jeff Sessions said in a statement. "When such actions arise from racial bigotry and hatred, they betray our core values and cannot be tolerated."

Some left-leaning Charlottesville organizers like Laura Goldblatt, a postdoctoral fellow at the University of Virginia, said that the full airing of such ideas would eventually lead more Americans to reject them. "I think this is the beginning of the end for this spectacularized part of the movement," Ms. Goldblatt said.

But some key far-right leaders say the outcome was exactly what they had hoped for.

"We achieved all of our objectives," Matthew Heimbach, a founder of the Nationalist Front, a neo-Nazi group that bills itself as an umbrella organization for the white nationalist movement, said in an interview Saturday. "We showed that our movement is not just online, but growing physically. We asserted ourselves as the voice of white America. We had zero vehicles damaged, all our people accounted for, and moved a large amount of men and materials in and out of the area. I think we did an incredibly impressive job."

Jason Kessler, a Charlottesville conservative and the main organizer of Saturday's rally, has been fighting for months against the City Council's plan to remove a statue of the Confederate general Robert E. Lee from Charlottesville's Emancipation Park, which once bore Lee's name.

Although he is a relative newcomer to the white nationalist movement, Mr. Kessler is well known in his hometown. He has attacked the city's status as a sanctuary for immigrants and has waged a public battle against Wes Bellamy, the black vice-mayor of Charlottesville and one of its city councilmen.

For weeks, a flier for the Unite the Right meeting made its way around the internet. It featured Pepe the Frog-styled soldiers bearing Confederate battle flags, and promised featured speakers like Mr. Spencer and Michael Hill, president of the Southern pro-secession group League of the South.

In Charlottesville, established groups like the local chapter of Black Lives Matter, as well as liberal and anarchist groups, started planning their response in June when activists learned that the Ku Klux Klan would be marching in the city — and that Mr. Kessler's rally would follow quickly after it, said Nathan Moore, who sits on the steering committee of Together Cville, a resistance group that formed shortly after the presidential election.

"It was all these different affinity groups that came together in the same place even if they didn't know each other before," Mr. Moore said. "It's been a real summer of hate here."

Heidi Beirich, who runs the intelligence project at the Southern Poverty Law Center, which monitors far-right groups, was among those who watched with alarm as the online excitement over the gathering grew. "It was astounding to see it go from 100 people saying they were going to go, to 300, to 500, to 700, to raising money on online platforms to facilitate that," she said.

Over the weekend, far-right groups poured into town, representing long-established racist organizations and the newer alt-right movement. It was not the first time these two strains had met up for a rally in recent months — members of both had appeared at a pro-Confederacy rally in New Orleans in May — but it was the latest example of a new bridging of two generations of hard-right sensibilities.

George Hawley, a University of Alabama political science professor who studies white supremacists, said that many of the far-right members he had interviewed did not inherit their racism from their parents, but developed it online. Many of them had never heard of, say, David Duke, the former Louisiana politician and former leader of the Ku Klux Klan.

But this weekend, Mr. Duke arrived in Charlottesville, along with an array of old-school and new-school white supremacists. They included organizations like Vanguard America, whose Nazi-era motto "Blood and Soil" was chanted by the marchers on Friday night, and the Rise Above Movement, a loose collective of California neo-Nazis, formerly known as the DIY Division, who train to fight at political events. Members of the League of the South showed up, as did their more recently radicalized colleagues from Identity Evropa, a white separatist group that endorses racial segregation.

On Friday night, hundreds of far-right sympathizers bearing torches marched across the University of Virginia campus, chanting "You will not replace us," and "Jews will not replace us." There was a brawl with counterprotesters, and at least one arrest.

Mr. Kessler said that the movement's torch-lit rally Friday night was especially successful. "It was a beautiful moment that no one will ever be able to take away from people who were involved."

The next morning, the trouble started early. Mr. Spencer recalled driving to Emancipation Park with Mr. Kessler. They arrived around 10:15 a.m., and were almost instantly met with dissent.

"As we were going in, I was sprayed with Mace," Mr. Spencer said. "Someone jumped out of the crowd and I got it in the face."

The counterprotesters included members of the local Charlottesville clergy and mainstream figures like the Harvard professor Cornel West. As the rally erupted into violence Saturday morning, the First United Methodist Church on East Jefferson Street opened its doors to demonstrators, serving cold water and offering basic medical care.

Dr. Hawley said he believed the far-left activists, known as antifa, were welcomed by the white nationalists. "I think to an extent the alt-right loves the antifa because they see them as being the perfect foil," he said.

But Ms. Goldblatt, while not addressing those leftists who resorted to violence, said that some kind of response in the street was necessary. History, she said, has shown that "ignoring white supremacy, in terms of shutting your doors and not coming out to confront them, has been a really dangerous strategy."

The scenes of violence were already dominating cable television news by 1:42 p.m., when a gray Dodge Challenger sped down a narrow street choked with counterprotesters. The driver, identified by the police as James Alex Fields Jr., had been seen at the protests alongside members of a right-wing group. He was charged with second-degree murder.

The organizers of the event distanced themselves from the crash and Mr. Kessler disavowed any knowledge of Mr. Fields. "I don't know anyone who knew," Mr. Kessler said. "Everyone in my circles was like, 'Who is this guy?' "

Lawrence Rosenthal, the executive director of the Berkeley Center for Right-Wing Studies at the University of California, said that Mr. Spencer appeared to welcome this level of violent, street-level politics. He noted an audio recording Mr. Spencer made after similar skirmishes in April in Berkeley. Mr. Spencer called them a "pitched battle" between two polarized, political "vanguards" that reminded him of political upheavals, presumably in Germany, that took place in the 1920s and 1930s.

"This is a very different dynamic than I'm used to," Mr. Spencer said. "I thought that political violence had just become impossible, that we'd never see it again."

Mr. Kessler was scheduled to address the news media Sunday. When he appeared, he was shouted down by protesters, and someone punched him.

After widespread criticism of Mr. Trump's remarks, an anonymous White House spokesperson on Sunday said in a statement that the president "condemns all forms of violence, bigotry and hatred. Of course that includes white supremacists, K.K.K. neo-Nazi and all extremist groups."

Preston Wiginton, a white nationalist from Texas, announced this weekend that he would hold a White Lives Matter rally at Texas A&M

on Sept. 11 with Mr. Spencer as a guest speaker. And on the neo-Nazi site The Daily Stormer, a post promised: “There will be more events. Soon. We are going to start doing this nonstop. Across the country.”

SHERYL GAY STOLBERG, **HAWES SPENCER** and **ALAN BLINDER** contributed reporting.

What Trump Got Wrong on Charlottesville

OPINION | BY ERICK-WOODS ERICKSON | AUG. 13, 2017

AS A CONSERVATIVE, I see both the social justice warrior alt-left and the white supremacist alt-right as two sides of the same coin. Both would punish others for wrongthink. Both see the other side not as opponents, but as evil that can justifiably be silenced. Both have risen in recent years as a response to the crumbling of Western civilization's certainties.

But white supremacists, not social justice warriors, were the ones marching with citronella-filled tiki torches in Charlottesville, Va. this weekend.

That is why it is perplexing that President Trump condemned the "egregious display of hatred, bigotry and violence on many sides — on many sides." A White House spokesman followed this up saying, "The president was condemning hatred, bigotry and violence from all sources and all sides. There was violence between protesters and counter protesters today."

That is all well and good, and I am glad he said something. But this is the same president who routinely mocked and attacked Barack Obama and Hillary Clinton for failing to call Islamic radicalism by its name. In Charlottesville, evil has a name, and it is white supremacy.

Our nation has an unfortunate history with white supremacy. Our founding creed declared that "all men are created equal," but it took much bloodshed for us to finally live up to that. Now, though, we do try to live up to our founding and belief that no race is superior to others.

The idea of white supremacy also has no place in science. We may be of different skin colors, ethnicities, heights, widths, eye colors and genders, but we are all part of the same human race. Out of the womb we are all equal, and equally in need of care. Theologically too, the

AL DRAGO FOR THE NEW YORK TIMES

President Trump spoke about the violence in Charlottesville, Va., at a previously scheduled event on health care for veterans on Saturday.

idea of a superior race is anathema to our Judeo-Christian heritage. Genesis 1 makes clear that all of us are created in God's image and likeness. To claim one race is superior to others is a sin against God, and Christians in the United States must forcefully condemn this.

Southerner whites bastardized the Bible in the 1800s claiming black skin color was the mark of Cain. It had no basis in the Bible. In fact, the story of Noah tells us that the line of Cain's descendants was wiped out in the great flood. Others claimed the "curse of Ham," but that too has no true basis in scripture.

Racial superiority is a repugnant idea and President Trump should condemn it by name. We should also note honestly that President Trump employs individuals who emboldened this movement. The president winked at and made kissy face with the alt-right as his advisers persuaded him it would be good politically. It is no coincidence that many of the men who marched in Charlottesville wore "Make America

Great Again" hats. This president and his advisers made a nefarious evil feel comfortable coming out of the shadows.

The Daily Stormer, a neo-Nazi publication, noted of President Trump's post-Charlottesville news conference that, "When asked to condemn, he just walked out of the room. Really, really good. God bless him." Silence and obfuscation in the face of evil only feeds evil. Naming and exposing evil forces it back into the shadows. The president who wanted Barack Obama to name radical Islam should take his own advice and be forceful. On a day that saw one person killed during the Charlottesville violence, the president did not need to play the "both sides are culpable" game. No side would be protesting in Charlottesville had not the white supremacists decided to march.

President Trump was elected at a time of great uncertainty. Both major political parties have become sclerotic and devoid of ideas. He offered up hope to people with real problems in this country. He offered real solutions and he promised he would fight. But it is more and more clear the president is incapable of learning on the job, rising to the occasion, or speaking with any conviction other than self-interest.

This president is our president. He is the president of the United States. But as we become less united as a nation, he seems unwilling or unable to speak with conviction and moral clarity. We will all be worse off for it.

Among the few bright lights in this weekend's darkness has been the moral clarity of our church leaders to stand against this evil. In the absence of a moral, capable leader, it is up to them to reclaim the moral center. As long as they continue to take that stand, there will be hope.

ERICK-WOODS ERICKSON is the editor of the website The Resurgent and a talk-show host on radio station WSB.

Far Right Plans Its Next Moves With a New Energy

BY ALAN FEUER | AUG. 14, 2017

THE WHITE SUPREMACISTS and right-wing extremists who came together over the weekend in Charlottesville, Va., are now headed home, many of them ready and energized, they said, to set their sights on bigger prizes.

Some were making arrangements to appear at future marches. Some were planning to run for public office. Others, taking a cue from the Charlottesville event — a protest, nominally, of the removal of a Confederate-era statue — were organizing efforts to preserve what they referred to as "white heritage" symbols in their home regions.

Calling it "an opportune time," Preston Wiginton, a Texas-based white nationalist, declared on Saturday that he planned to hold a "White Lives Matter" march on Sept. 11 on the campus of Texas A&M — with a keynote speaker, Richard B. Spencer, who was featured at the Charlottesville event.

Mr. Wiginton was not the only one seeking to capitalize on the weekend's events. On Monday, Augustus Sol Invictus, a conservative Florida lawyer who changed his name from Austin Gillespie, and attended the "Unite the Right" rally in Virginia, said he planned to announce on Tuesday that he would seek Florida's Republican nomination for the Senate. And at a news conference on Monday, Mr. Spencer, a prominent white supremacist, promised to return to Charlottesville for another rally. "There is no way in hell that I am not going back," he said.

The far right, which has returned to prominence in the past year or so, has always been an amalgam of factions and causes, some with pro-Confederate or neo-Nazi leanings, some opposed to political correctness or feminism. But the Charlottesville event, the largest of its kind in recent years, exposed the pre-existing fault lines in the movement.

The ugliness of the rally — which included crowds of young white men offering the Nazi salute and which led to the death of a woman

ALEX WROBLEWSKI FOR THE NEW YORK TIMES

Richard B. Spencer, center, a prominent white nationalist, held a news conference at his office in Alexandria, Va., on Monday. He was joined by Nathan Damigo, right, the founder of Identity Evropa, a white separatist group.

in a car attack — has resulted in a fracture on the right. After waiting days, for instance, to directly criticize the extremist groups, President Trump on Monday condemned white supremacists, saying from the White House that "racism is evil."

Some hard-line conservatives beat Mr. Trump to the punch, apparently concluding that the marchers had gone too far and that their aggressiveness and messages could hurt the movement. Mike Cernovich, an influential right-wing media figure who is hardly shy of controversy, posted a Twitter message on Saturday afternoon, attacking what the self-proclaimed alt-right, parts of which use Nazi imagery and racist language, had become.

"The alt-right will now be made up of losers with nothing to lose," he wrote. "This sets ceiling on numbers while also attracting loons and terrorists."

Unwilling to be associated with explicit neo-Nazis, some of those invited to the Charlottesville event did not even bother showing up. Among them was Gavin McInnes, the founder of the Proud Boys, a conservative fraternal organization of self-described "Western chauvinists" that has engaged in several battles with the left in recent months.

Well before the gathering in Charlottesville, Mr. McInnes had planned to hold a "Free Speech" rally in Boston on Saturday, but it remained unclear whether it would take place after civil rights groups on Monday asked the city's mayor, Martin J. Walsh, to revoke the rally's permit. Mr. McInnes, in an unusual move, said he hoped the event would be canceled.

"It's a lose-lose situation," he explained. "If we have a permit and we don't go, it would show that antifa" — or anti-fascists — "can shut us down whenever they want. But if we do go, it will look like we're fighting for Nazis we don't like."

On Monday night, officials at Texas A&M announced that they were canceling Mr. Wiginton's event. But he pushed back, saying he would fight the university in court. "It seems like the First Amendment doesn't apply to white people," he said.

Elsewhere in the country, other movement leaders were busy pushing forward with their plans. Jack Posobiec, an activist who interrupted a June performance of "Julius Caesar" in New York that portrayed the assassinated leader much like Mr. Trump, is planning to march on Google's New York headquarters on Saturday to protest the company's firing of an employee who criticized its diversity policy.

Matthew Heimbach, a founder of the Nationalist Front, an umbrella organization for the white nationalist movement, said on Monday that he was going to start organizing against an effort to remove two Confederate statues from public squares in Lexington, Ky. As the violence broke out in Charlottesville on Saturday, the mayor of Lexington, Jim Gray, wrote on Twitter that the statues should come down.

And Eli Mosley, an organizer for Identity Evropa, a white separatist group that endorses racial segregation, said that his and other like-minded groups planned to hold more rallies in Virginia. Indeed, on Monday, a Confederate heritage organization filed a request with state officials to hold an event on Sept. 16 near a monument of Robert E. Lee in Richmond. Mr. Mosley was so enthused by the Charlottesville rally that he claimed the movement could within two years attract as many as 10,000 people to a national march in Washington.

"Every city needs to watch out," Mr. Mosley said. "We are everywhere."

Mr. Mosley added that he had no concerns about the president's remarks and that they would have no effect on the movement's future plans.

"The president is being advised by people who don't know what's going on," Mr. Mosley added. "He's essentially going off of false information. We're not in any way worried about moving forward."

Mr. Heimbach echoed that notion, saying that the president's remarks would not stop him or his colleagues. "I expected him to backtrack," he added. "You have Republicans and Democrats united in the purpose of genociding our people. With the pressure put on Mr. Trump, I'm not surprised he made those comments."

The goals of the far right have never been uniform. The disparate factions of the movement have sometimes come together in supporting concrete issues like restricting immigration and creating "a white ethnostate" in America. But at their large-scale rallies like the one in Charlottesville, they are often mainly interested in solidifying their communal bonds and attracting the attention of the news media.

Mr. Gillespie is among a handful of people to have taken the traditional route of seeking office. (He ran a failed campaign for the Senate last year as a Libertarian candidate in Florida.) While one of Mr. Heimbach's groups, the Traditionalist Worker Party, has also run candidates, mostly for local offices, it is arguably more concerned with creating a grass-roots movement of white nationalists. The group has organized on behalf of disaffected coal miners and those affected by the opioid epidemic, and it has handed out white supremacist literature at gun shows and neighborhood Christmas events.

Like other white supremacists, Mr. Spencer has called for "a white homeland" in North America. But he, too, can often seem less interested in policy than in headlines.

At his news conference, he referred — cheekily, it seemed — to the throngs in Charlottesville who marched by torchlight in an echo of the Ku Klux Klan.

"The idea that the K.K.K. had a monopoly on torches," he said, "that is not the case."

SHERYL GAY STOLBERG and **NICHOLAS FANDOS** contributed reporting.

Before 'Unite the Right' Rally, Trump Does Not Condemn Supremacists

BY NOAH WEILAND | AUG. 11, 2018

WASHINGTON — As white nationalists planned to gather in front of the White House on Sunday to mark the anniversary of last year's violent rally in Charlottesville, Va., President Trump denounced "all types of racism," but did not specifically condemn the supremacists.

"Riots in Charlottesville a year ago resulted in senseless death and division," he wrote on Twitter on Saturday morning. "We must come together as a nation. I condemn all types of racism and acts of violence. Peace to ALL Americans!"

Mr. Trump's general call for unity, as Washington braced for the possibility of violence between the white nationalists and counterdemonstrators, echoed his reluctance a year ago after the deadly Charlottesville rally to single out the supremacists for condemnation.

In what is seen as a defining mark of his presidency, he blamed "both sides" for the violence, eliciting widespread criticism for what was seen as drawing a moral equivalence between hate groups — some of whom supported his candidacy — and those who protested them.

Accusations of racism have shadowed Mr. Trump over his decades as a real estate mogul, reality television star and president. Those claims have been renewed in recent weeks as he has questioned the intelligence of prominent black people such as LeBron James and Representative Maxine Waters and criticized professional football players for kneeling during the national anthem.

In a new memoir, Omarosa Manigault Newman, a former White House adviser tasked with outreach to African-Americans, claims that the president regularly used a racial slur while he was the host of the show "Celebrity Apprentice," though she never heard him say it herself. Asked by a reporter about the book on Saturday at his club in

Bedminster, N.J., the president held a hand to his mouth, as if to whisper, and said: "Lowlife. She's a lowlife."

The rally on Sunday, called Unite the Right II, is scheduled to take over Lafayette Square for two hours in the evening. Officers from the United States Park Police and the Washington police department will erect a barrier separating the white nationalists and the thousands of counterprotesters who intend to oppose them.

The Unite the Right group plans to have up to 400 people at the rally, according to the permit it received from the National Park Service, though the number in attendance could be considerably smaller. An antiracism group, the Answer Coalition, was granted a permit in Lafayette Square for a group more than three times the size of Unite the Right's. Other groups of counterprotesters have permits to gather elsewhere in the city.

Jason Kessler, who helped organize last year's Charlottesville rally, is scheduled to speak to the crowd, as is David Duke, the former politician and Ku Klux Klan leader.

The Park Service granted a routine First Amendment demonstration permit to Mr. Kessler. "In anyone's recollection, there has never been a First Amendment permit that's been denied," said Mike Litterst, a Park Service spokesman.

Last year in Charlottesville, neo-Nazis, Ku Klux Klansmen and other members of hate groups marched through the University of Virginia campus shouting anti-Semitic slogans, then fought with counterprotesters in the city streets. A man who espoused neo-Nazi views drove his vehicle into the counterdemonstators, killing a 32-year-old woman, Heather D. Heyer.

The chance of that kind of spontaneous mayhem has led to weeks of planning between Washington's law enforcement agencies, which have developed proposals to guard marches leading to the rally and the rally itself, as well as deal with any confrontations that precede or follow it in the streets of Washington.

Sgt. James Dingeldein of the Park Police said his agency, the Washington police and the Park Service had met with Mr. Kessler and leaders of counterprotest groups to explain to them what is permissible on the grounds of the park. The Park Service has issued a detailed set of limits and prohibitions on items that can be brought in, banning some of the items that were wielded in Charlottesville.

"If there is potential for violence, it will be dealt with quickly," Sergeant Dingeldein said. Mr. Kessler said last month that he would discourage those attending from acting violently.

Federal officials have expressed concern that violence could spill into downtown streets once the rally has dispersed and its participants may feel less inhibited. Sergeant Dingeldein said the police agencies had riot control teams that could be deployed.

James Murray, an assistant director in the Secret Service's Office of Protective Operations, warned in a letter on Monday to the Park Service that some of the same counterprotesters who seized downtown streets at the presidential inauguration in January 2017 were also interested in Sunday's demonstrations, and were "known to have engaged in violent and destructive activity."

"Violence can commonly occur between highly charged groups of protesters and counterprotesters," Mr. Murray wrote. Members of the sometimes violent movement known as antifa are expected to be among the counterprotesters on Sunday.

Muriel E. Bowser, the Washington mayor, activated the city's emergency operations center on Thursday. Although no rally is planned in Charlottesville this weekend, Gov. Ralph Northam of Virginia declared a state of emergency. Police officers in Charlottesville had put up metal barriers by Saturday morning to cut off access to downtown streets.

"We have people coming to our city for the sole purpose of spewing hate," Ms. Bowser said at a news conference on Thursday. "It didn't make sense last year, and it doesn't make sense now."

MAGGIE HABERMAN contributed reporting from Bedminster, N.J.

Rally by White Nationalists Was Over Almost Before It Began

BY RICHARD FAUSSET | AUG. 12, 2018

WASHINGTON — After weeks of hype, white supremacists managed to muster just a couple of dozen supporters on Sunday in the nation's capital for the first anniversary of their deadly rally in Charlottesville, Va., finding themselves greatly outnumbered by counterprotesters, police officers and representatives of the news media.

There appeared to be many reasons for the poor showing from a movement that just a year ago turned out hundreds of adherents who boldly marched unmasked in Charlottesville, chanting anti-Semitic slogans and bearing torches.

The alt-right movement, never very well unified, has been particularly rived by infighting and schisms in the last year. Members have been outed by both online activists and mainstream media outlets, causing some to lose their jobs. The left's ability to turn out counterprotesters has also been a factor, from the hard-left activists threatening violence against far-right street protesters, to center-left citizens who have been vocal, and explicit, in expressing their disgust and scorn.

In an interview on Monday, right-wing agitator Jason Kessler, the organizer of Sunday's event in Washington, said that fear and an "atmosphere of intimidation" were the primary reasons for the sparse turnout.

For example, he said that participants in a chat group on Discord, a digital communications app favored by the far right, were harassed in the run-up to the rally after their personal information, including phone numbers, addresses and license plates, was released online.

Other leaders painted a picture of an alt-right that is currently in disarray, lacking unity and a coherent strategy. "We are facing so much pushback that people are not in the mood to celebrate," said Richard B. Spencer, a white nationalist leader who was a prominent figure at last year's Charlottesville rally, in an interview on Monday.

ERIN SCHAFF FOR THE NEW YORK TIMES

Protesters marching toward downtown Charlottesville on Sunday.

He demonstrated the divisions within the alt-right's leadership by calling Mr. Kessler "one of the problems" with Sunday's rally. "He is not the person to follow," Mr. Spencer said. "He jumps on this whole bandwagon late and does not have a lot of authenticity."

Even with the low turnout on Sunday, almost no one walked away with the sense that the nation's divisions were any closer to healing.

Indeed, the streets of downtown Washington were charged with tension, emotion and noise, particularly in the afternoon, as Mr. Kessler and perhaps 20 fellow members of the far right — some wearing bright red "Make America Great Again" hats, some draped in American flags — marched under heavy police escort from the Metro station in the Foggy Bottom neighborhood to their barricaded and heavily protected rally area near the White House.

They were surrounded by a vast, rolling plume of counterprotesters, who hurled insults, waved middle fingers and chanted "Shame!"

"You killed a girl in Charlottesville!" one voice in the crowd yelled, referring to Heather Heyer, a woman who was fatally injured a year ago when a man who espoused white supremacist views rammed his car into a crowd of counterprotesters.

A similar dynamic to the one in Washington played out in Charlottesville on Sunday, where few if any far-right demonstrators could be found, and where the most palpable tensions developed between left-wing protesters and the police, whose presence in the city was heavy and, some argued, heavy-handed.

"The problem is, the only opposition is the police," said Pastor Robert Lewis of the Hinton Avenue United Methodist Church, as he and a group of religious representatives stood facing rows of officers in an effort to form what he called a buffer between them and the protesters.

Only a handful of arrests were reported in Charlottesville on Sunday, including a man and a woman who got into a fistfight after the man saluted the town's statue of Robert E. Lee. By early evening, the security cordon around the downtown area had been lifted, hours ahead of schedule.

In Washington, the mere threat of another large turnout from the far right, coupled with a large turnout from the far left — among them, hundreds of black-clad, masked and helmeted anti-fascist protesters known as antifa — seemed to indicate that the United States was not over its turn toward European-style politics by street protest.

It was also a return to the way extreme-right demonstrations in America tended to play out before Charlottesville.

The template starts when a group like the Ku Klux Klan announces a rally. Next comes news coverage, fevered and intense. That prompts a huge number of activists, police officers and everyday people to turn out, dwarfing what is often a pathetically small band of extremists in hoods or armbands.

That does not mean that hate is on the wane. According to the Center for the Study of Hate and Extremism, there were a total of 1,038 hate crimes recorded in the 10 largest American cities last year, an increase of 12 percent from 2016 and the highest figure in more than a decade.

HILARY SWIFT FOR THE NEW YORK TIMES

A counterprotester in Washington on Sunday.

In Washington on Sunday, the far-right rally felt as though it was over before it had really begun. It was officially scheduled to start at 5:30 p.m., but the small band of extremists arrived early, finished their demonstration and left before that time.

Another factor was a thunderstorm that rolled over Washington around 5 p.m., dampening enthusiasm and thinning out the crowds. As the rain began falling in earnest, the white supremacists began leaving Lafayette Park in front of the White House.

Counterprotesters in the park booed them, chanting “na-na-na-na, hey hey, goodbye,” and their mood soon grew celebratory.

Many Washingtonians felt a sense of relief that the event did not turn into something worse — and that the bad guys had effectively lost.

“I have no problem with them and their protest,” said Ianta Summers, a counterprotester carrying a large Black Lives Matter flag. “I have a problem with their ideals, and this just shows them, you can show up and speak, but you have to deal with the consequences.”

At the same time, some saw in the wall-to-wall media coverage a kind of public relations victory for the far right. "They are getting international coverage and profiles, and the bottom line is that exposure equals importance," said Brian H. Levin, director of the Center for the Study of Hate and Extremism at California State University, San Bernardino.

Mr. Levin added that there had been "over-coverage" and "hype" in the run-up to the protests. "And at a time when the movement is in disarray and some of its members are getting knocked off of social media, it can, nonetheless, get a message out across millions of eyeballs on television and in print," he said.

In the run-up to the rally, the Washington police had prepared meticulously to avoid violence. In the area around the White House, placards bearing the name of Police Chief Peter Newsham had appeared on light posts as though the nation's capital were a dusty Wild West town: "All Firearms Prohibited Within 1,000 Feet of This Sign." The rule was in effect from 6 a.m. to midnight.

The weapons ban, justified by a section of District of Columbia code, echoed a similar move by the New Orleans police last year as they prepared for a showdown between left and right over a plan to remove Confederate statues there.

Just as importantly, the Washington police kept the two factions strictly separated throughout the afternoon, using barricades, their bodies and motorcycles.

Most of the counterprotesters could not even catch sight of the brief right-wing rally, where some of the roughly two dozen demonstrators inside their penned-off area held signs that said, "Protect the Endangered Species, Stop White Genocide," and "White Lives Matter."

Mr. Kessler, speaking to the small group of marchers he was with in Lafayette Square, said that he did not want antifa counterprotesters "using violence to shut down the speech of people they disagree with."

He tried to account for his group's meager showing by acknowledging that some of his fellow white nationalists were fearful of the reception they would receive.

"There were a lot of people who were at last year's rally who are very scared this year," he said. "They felt like last year they came to express their point of view. They were attacked. And when they fought back, they were overly prosecuted."

The antifa forces, numbering perhaps a few hundred, pooled around the Old Executive Office Building under a banner that declared, "It takes a bullet to bash a fash." But with no object of their ire in sight, they seemed vaguely lost. A few tried to set a Confederate battle flag ablaze, but it would not catch fire, and they had to settle for pulling it apart and stomping it.

At one point, some in the crowd took a right turn, while others moved forward on 17th Street, but seemed unsure where to go next.

For many of the counterprotesters, there was a kind of weariness that they had been compelled yet again to show up, as a kind of visual and numerical riposte to the forces of intolerance and hate.

"I can't believe I have to protest Nazis in 2018," read one sign early Sunday afternoon at a rally in Freedom Plaza.

Jessica Balaschak, 43, a graphic designer, was one of the hundreds in the crowd. She had come from New York City with a sign she recycled from a spontaneous protest at Trump Tower last year.

"There aren't 'many sides,' " it declared, a response to President Trump's much-derided comment last year that seemed to lay the blame for the Charlottesville violence at the feet of both right-wing extremists and counterprotesters.

Ms. Balaschak said she hoped to help show the country that "we're not O.K. with this at all," meaning the white nationalists and the president who she believes has emboldened them.

"They're so confident that the government supports their views that they're marching around showing their faces in public," she said. "This isn't like arguing over the marginal tax rate. This is a very black-and-white situation."

Among the speakers at a counter rally was Dr. Harriette Wimms, an activist and psychologist from Baltimore. She led a chant of "love wins" as a protester to her right held up a sign that read "Give Nazis a Platform" — and showed a bloody guillotine on a platform.

Ms. Wimms, 50, an African-American, spoke of the overt racism and discrimination that older members of her family had experienced in the past, and how, as a younger woman, she had argued with her parents that times had changed — that a new generation of Americans had renounced bigotry, and that they should no longer be "a little leery of white people."

But recent events, she said, had complicated her view. Now, she felt that both she and her parents had been right.

Fascism persists in America, she said. But "we are still here, and we will stand strong in love."

HAWES SPENCER and **MICHAEL WINES** contributed reporting from Charlottesville, Va.; **CATIE EDMONDSON**, **GARDINER HARRIS** and **NOAH WEILAND** from Washington; **FARAH STOCKMAN** from Boston; and **SERGE KOVALESKI** and **ALAN FEUER** from New York.

A Year After Charlottesville, Disarray in the White Supremacist Movement

BY RICHARD FAUSSET, SERGE F. KOVALESKI AND ALAN FEUER | AUG. 13, 2018

WASHINGTON — The white supremacists who alarmed the nation a year ago on the streets of Charlottesville, Va., with their tiki torches and hateful chants show signs, at least temporarily, of being pushed back into the shadows after months of legal challenges, counterprotests and internal strife.

Sunday's sparse turnout on the streets of Washington says little about the country's current levels of intolerance, bigotry and xenophobia. Hate crimes in the 10 largest American cities were up last year, and fearmongering talk of "massive demographic changes" has made its way into the mainstream. But it does say something about the disarray within a movement that last August had a disquietingly large turnout at a Unite the Right rally in Charlottesville.

"It was a dead-enders event from the get-go, meaning that Charlottesville a year ago had an intention and agenda, and both failed," said Lawrence Rosenthal, chairman of the Berkeley Center For Right-Wing Studies. "And the coalition that came together to put it together dissolved."

The view from those inside the movement is not that different. "Now, we are facing so much pushback that people are not in the mood to celebrate," said Richard B. Spencer, the white nationalist and prominent alt-right figure, who declined to attend Sunday's event. "And I'm not going to do something demoralizing."

The coalition of old-school racist groups, neo-Confederates and Internet-savvy white identitarians that brought about last year's rally has proved, in the months since, to be a disparate herd that cannot agree on a leader or a particular brand of intolerance. Mobilizing large numbers of white supremacists in public appears to be a challenge, even though nobody would ever say they have gone away. In fact, their discriminatory messages are now echoed by some politicians and commentators.

Sunday's Washington rally — which was dwarfed by thousands of counterdemonstrators — was arranged by Jason Kessler, 34, one of numerous people who had a hand in planning last year's torch-lit rally and, later, violent protests in the streets. On Twitter, he has obscenely mocked Heather Heyer, the young woman who was killed when a man who espoused white supremacist views rammed his car into counter-protesters at the Charlottesville rally.

On Sunday, under heavy police escort, Mr. Kessler marched defiantly through the streets of Washington, holding an American flag while flanked by a small group of supporters, some in the "Make America Great Again" ball caps favored by backers of President Trump.

But in a sign of the fracturing of the alt-right, before, during and after the Sunday rally, hard-core racists and neo-Nazis, whom Mr. Kessler has publicly disavowed, took to social media to attack him and this weekend's protest, which was billed as a second Unite the Right event. Many of those attacks took place on Gab, an online forum to which many on the alt-right migrated after they were kicked off Twitter.

The attacks came from both well-known members of the alt-right and from anonymous followers. Their argument, in essence, was that Mr. Kessler was not extreme enough.

One Gab poster, who identified himself as Sterben, said that Mr. Kessler should have been more welcoming to Nazis and other such groups "because there's more of us and history is never on the side of the cowards."

A week before the event in Washington, Andrew Anglin, who runs the neo-Nazi website The Daily Stormer, published an article titled, "Don't Go to Unite the Right 2 — We Disavow."

"We cannot win a battle on the streets," Mr. Anglin wrote.

Instead, he counseled taking part in events like "Stormer Book Clubs," where followers "can get together with other people who think like we do in real life."

AL DRAGO FOR THE NEW YORK TIMES

Sunday's alt-right rally in Washington was dwarfed by thousands of counter-demonstrators.

"We need to remain in the realm of the hip, cool, sexy, fun," Mr. Anglin wrote. "We need to speak to the culture. We do not want the image of being a bunch of weird losers who march around" while "completely outnumbered and get mocked by the entire planet."

One significant headache for the far right is a federal lawsuit, filed in October, that accuses organizers of last year's rally, including Mr. Spencer and Mr. Kessler, of encouraging followers to arm themselves and commit acts of violence. Organized by Roberta A. Kaplan, a New York lawyer, the civil conspiracy action is modeled on an earlier suit that helped take down the Nuremberg Files, a website that listed the names of abortion providers.

"It's purposeful. It's being done to break groups like us," said Jeff Schoep, national commander of the National Socialist Movement, which participated in the Charlottesville rally but steered clear of Sunday's event.

AL DRAGO FOR THE NEW YORK TIMES

Jason Kessler, center, one of several people who had a hand in planning last year's torch-lit rally in Charlottesville, Va., marched on Sunday.

Some observers believe the suit could expose the murky funding of some of the alt-right groups. But the effort to expose them has extended beyond the courtroom and the news media.

In late July, in anticipation of this year's rally, activists posted personal information of organizers online and encouraged people to alert employers of their affiliations, put up fliers outing them in their neighborhoods, and uncover their "ties to more 'respectable' right-wing organizations that help them hide their true intentions."

Mr. Kessler said that participants in a chat group on Discord, a digital communications app favored by the far right, were harassed in the run-up to the rally after their personal information, including phone numbers, addresses and license plates, were released online.

Mr. Kessler provided no proof of such harassment. But pushback to the alt-right in the streets of Washington was in plain view. The area around the White House was thick Sunday with counterprotesters

HILARY SWIFT FOR THE NEW YORK TIMES

A protest sign after the "Unite the Right" rally in Lafayette Square in Washington on Sunday.

who were vocal in their contempt and disgust for the movement. They were joined by members of the far-left antifa movement, who marched with helmets and masked faces behind a banner threatening violence toward fascists.

James Anderson, an editor at ItsGoingDown.org, an anarchist-inflected website that has become a kind of clearinghouse for writing about antifa, said that after Charlottesville, young people from groups like Black Lives Matter and the Democratic Socialists of America began to work with masked and black-clad anti-fascists to combat the rise of the alt-right.

"Their worst nightmare has come to pass," Mr. Anderson added, referring to the alt-right. "Young people, especially across racial lines, are working together against the far right."

But some experts on white nationalism say the movement's political agenda remains disconcertingly widespread. And some policy issues the far right has promoted, including immigration restrictions, ending affirmative action and instituting trade protections, have been embraced by mainstream right-wing politicians and pundits.

"What's crucial for the fate of the alt-right is not the demonstrations," said Thomas J. Main, a political scientist at Baruch College. "They are a political movement that is concerned with influencing the way people think, and there are a lot of signs that their ideas continue to penetrate mainstream media and political culture."

In "The Rise of the Alt-Right," published by the Brookings Institution, Dr. Main tracked web traffic to 10 sites associated with the alt-right. After Charlottesville, visits plummeted to The Daily Stormer, one of the most popular sites, which had trouble finding an internet company to host it.

But overall traffic remained relatively high through February of this year, the most recent time period available, Dr. Main said, collectively hovering around four million visits on average per month — a bit more than the liberal magazine The New Republic.

RICHARD FAUSSET reported from Washington, and **SERGE KOVALESKI** and **ALAN FEUER** from New York. **AMY HARMON** contributed reporting from New York.

Jury Recommends Life in Prison for James Fields in Fatal Charlottesville Attack

BY JULIA JACOBS | DEC. 11, 2018

A JURY RECOMMENDED on Tuesday that a demonstrator who drove into a crowd of counterprotesters at last year's white nationalist rally in Charlottesville, Va., killing a woman, spend the rest of his life in prison.

The recommendation came four days after the jury convicted the man, James Fields Jr., 21, of first-degree murder in the attack, which also injured nearly 40 other people. Mr. Fields was also convicted of nine other charges, including aggravated malicious wounding and leaving the scene of a fatal accident, for which the jury recommended a sentence of hundreds more years in prison.

The jury's action on Tuesday is not a final verdict. Under Virginia law, it serves as a recommendation to the judge, who will decide the sentence.

Judge Richard E. Moore of Charlottesville Circuit Court will sentence Mr. Fields at the end of March, said Brian Wheeler, a spokesman for the city. He can order a weaker sentence than what the jury proposed, but not a stronger one.

In August 2017, Mr. Fields traveled from Ohio to attend the Unite the Right rally, where swastika-toting white supremacists swarmed the streets and clashed with counterprotesters. In an attack that killed a 32-year-old woman, Heather Heyer, Mr. Fields sped down a narrow street packed with counterprotesters, many who were on their way home after the authorities shut down the demonstration.

The jury's complete sentence recommendation included life in prison for first-degree murder, as well as 419 years of prison time and hundreds of thousands of dollars in fines for the lesser charges. Mr.

Fields faces a second trial on federal hate crime charges, which could result in the death penalty.

"In the end, the hands of justice say that he needs to be kept away from society for a while, and I'm content with that," Susan Bro, Ms. Heyer's mother, told reporters at a news conference outside the court on Tuesday.

At the conference, Joseph D. Platania, the commonwealth's attorney, praised the jury's decision, calling it a "true act of public service." During the trial, prosecutors had argued that Mr. Fields traveled to the rally with an intent to commit harm, citing a cartoon that he shared on Instagram months before the protests that showed a car ramming into a crowd.

Video footage from the episode showed Mr. Fields's Dodge Challenger idling and then reversing before accelerating into the group of pedestrians.

A lawyer for Mr. Fields did not immediately respond to a request for comment on Tuesday. In court, the defense team argued that Mr. Fields did not travel to Charlottesville with the intention of doing harm and said he "acted out of fear."

Organizers chose Charlottesville as the site of the Unite the Right rally as a rebuke to the proposed removal of monuments to Confederate generals in the city. The protests started on the University of Virginia campus with a march of hundreds of torch-bearing demonstrators, many of them shouting phrases like, "You will not replace us," and "Jews will not replace us."

That initial demonstration prompted hundreds of counterprotesters to converge the next day, setting up tense confrontations with the white nationalist demonstrators that culminated at the end of the day with Mr. Fields's deadly attack.

FARAH STOCKMAN contributed reporting.

Glossary

agitator A person who incites others to rebellious actions or protest.

agrarian Relating to the cultivating of land or farming.

alt-right A loosely defined term that relates to groups of white nationalists, white supremacists, neo-fascists and other far-right fringe groups.

Antifa A political protest movement connected by groups militantly opposed to fascism and other forms of far-right ideology.

anti-Semitism Hostility toward or prejudice against Jews.

balkanize To divide a region or a body into smaller, hostile groups.

chauvinist Showing excessive support or prejudice toward one group; an attitude of superiority toward the opposite sex.

Confederate Relating to the Confederate States of America, the unrecognized country made up of Southern states between 1861-1865.

demographics Statistical data referring to population and groups within it.

ethnostate A state in which citizenship is restricted toward members of a particular racial or ethnic group.

eugenics The science of trying to improve or alter a population by controlling breeding in order to increase certain desirable characteristics and to decrease others.

fascism A political philosophy characterized by dictatorial power that places emphasis on nation and race above individual interests.

misogyny Dislike of, contempt for or prejudice toward women.

moral equivalence A term used in political discourse to imply that a fair comparison can be made between two sides of a conflict.

nationalist A person who strongly identifies with their own nation and supports its best interest to the detriment of other nations.

neo-Nazism Political or social movements intended to restore and implement the ideology of Nazism.

noxious Harmful, toxic or very unpleasant.

propaganda Information, particularly of a misleading nature, used to promote a particular political point of view.

Rhodesia A country in the south of Africa from 1965-1979 that was ruled by white British colonizers.

segregationist Advocating for the forced seperation of different racial groups.

white nationalist A type of nationalism that seeks to create a state for white people and to develop a unified white national identity.

white supremacy The racist belief that white people are superior to other races and therefore should be dominant over them.

Media Literacy Terms

"Media literacy" refers to the ability to access, understand, critically assess and create media. The following terms are important components of media literacy, and they will help you critically engage with the articles in this title.

angle The aspect of a news story that a journalist focuses on and develops.

attribution The method by which a source is identified or by which facts and information are assigned to the person who provided them.

balance Principle of journalism that both perspectives of an argument should be presented in a fair way.

bias A disposition of prejudice in favor of a certain idea, person or perspective.

credibility The quality of being trustworthy and believable, said of a journalistic source.

editorial Article of opinion or interpretation.

fake news A fictional or made-up story presented in the style of a legitimate news story, intended to deceive readers; also commonly used to criticize legitimate news because of its perspective or unfavorable coverage of a subject.

human interest story A type of story that focuses on individuals and how events or issues affect their life, generally offering a sense of relatability to the reader.

impartiality Principle of journalism that a story should not reflect a journalist's bias and should contain balance.

intention The motive or reason behind something, such as the publication of a news story.

interview story A type of story in which the facts are gathered primarily by interviewing another person or persons.

motive The reason behind something, such as the publication of a news story or a source's perspective on an issue.

news story An article or style of expository writing that reports news, generally in a straightforward fashion and without editorial comment.

op-ed An opinion piece that reflects a prominent individual's opinion on a topic of interest.

paraphrase The summary of an individual's words, with attribution, rather than a direct quotation of their exact words.

plagiarism An attempt to pass another person's work as one's own without attribution.

quotation The use of an individual's exact words indicated by the use of quotation marks and proper attribution.

reliability The quality of being dependable and accurate, said of a journalistic source.

rhetorical device Technique in writing intending to persuade the reader or communicate a message from a certain perspective.

source The origin of the information reported in journalism.

style A distinctive use of language in writing or speech; also a news or publishing organization's rules for consistent use of language with regard to spelling, punctuation, typography and capitalization, usually regimented by a house style guide.

tone A manner of expression in writing or speech.

Media Literacy Questions

1. Identify the various sources cited in the article "White Nationalists Celebrate 'an Awakening' After Donald Trump's Victory" (on page 131). How do the journalists attribute information to each of these sources in their article? How effective are their attributions in helping the reader identify their sources?

2. In "Why the Announcement of a Looming White Minority Makes Demographers Nervous" (on page 47), Sabrina Tavernise paraphrases information from Jennifer Richeson. What are the strengths of the use of a paraphrase as opposed to a direct quote? What are the weaknesses?

3. Compare the headlines of "White Supremacists' Use of Campus Propaganda Is Soaring, Report Finds" (on page 78) and "The Housewives of White Supremacy" (on page 34). Which is a more compelling headline, and why? How could the less compelling headline be changed to better draw the reader's interest?

4. Does Richard Fausset demonstrate the journalistic principle of balance in his article "A Voice of Hate in America's Heartland" (on page 116)? If so, how did he do so? If not, what could he have included to make his article more balanced?

5. The article "What Trump Got Wrong on Charlottesville" (on page 185) is an example of an op-ed. Identify how Erick-Woods Erickson's attitude and tone help convey his opinion on the topic.

6. Does "Far-Right Groups Surge Into National View in Charlottesville" (on page 179) use multiple sources? What are the strengths of using multiple sources in a journalistic piece? What are the weaknesses of relying heavily on only one or a few sources?

7. What is the intention of the article "What White Nationalism Gets Right About American History" (on page 22)? How effectively does it achieve its intended purpose?

8. Analyze the authors' reporting in "University of Florida Braces for Richard Spencer" (on page 59) and "White Nationalists Love Corey Stewart. He Keeps Them Close." (on page 148). Do you think the reporting in one article is more impartial than in the other? If so, why do you think so?

9. " 'The Daily' Transcript: Interview With Former White Nationalist Derek Black" (on page 97) is an example of an interview. Can you identify skills or techniques used by Michael Barbaro to gather information from Derek Black?

Citations

All citations in this list are formatted according to the Modern Language Association's (MLA) style guide.

BOOK CITATION

THE NEW YORK TIMES EDITORIAL STAFF. *White Nationalists: Who Are They and What Do They Believe?* New York: New York Times Educational Publishing, 2020.

ONLINE ARTICLE CITATIONS

ASTOR, MAGGIE. "White Supremacists Are Increasingly Using Public Banners." *The New York Times*, 15 Mar. 2018, https://www.nytimes.com/2018/03/15/us/white-supremacist-banners-adl.html.

BLACK, R. DEREK. "What White Nationalism Gets Right About American History." *The New York Times*, 19 Aug. 2017, https://www.nytimes.com/2017/08/19/opinion/sunday/white-nationalism-american-history-statues.html.

BLOW, CHARLES M. "Trump's Potent Toxicity." *The New York Times*, 28 Oct. 2018, https://www.nytimes.com/2018/10/28/opinion/trump-toxicity-pittsburgh-violence.html.

CAULEY, KASHANA. "The State of the (White Nationalist) Union." *The New York Times*, 31 Jan. 2018, https://www.nytimes.com/2018/01/31/opinion/state-white-nationalist-union.html.

EDMONDSON, CATIE. "Standing 'Against White Supremacy,' G.O.P. Campaign Chief Rebukes Steve King." *The New York Times*, 30 Oct. 2018, https://www.nytimes.com/2018/10/30/us/politics/steve-king-white-supremacy.html.

ENZINNA, WES. "Renouncing Hate: What Happens When a White Nationalist Repents." *The New York Times*, 10 Sept. 2018, https://www.nytimes.com/2018/09/10/books/review/eli-saslow-rising-out-of-hatred.html.

ERICKSON, ERICK-WOODS. "What Trump Got Wrong on Charlottesville." *The New York Times*, 13 Aug. 2017, https://www.nytimes.com/2017/08/13/opinion/trump-charlottesville-white-supremacy.html.

FAUSSET, RICHARD. "I Interviewed a White Nationalist and Fascist. What Was I Left With?" *The New York Times*, 25 Nov. 2017, https://www.nytimes.com/2017/11/25/insider/white-nationalist-interview-questions.html.

FAUSSET, RICHARD. "Rally by White Nationalists Was Over Almost Before It Began." *The New York Times*, 12 Aug. 2018, https://www.nytimes.com/2018/08/12/us/politics/charlottesville-va-protest-unite-the-right.html.

FAUSSET, RICHARD. "A Voice of Hate in America's Heartland." *The New York Times*, 25 Nov. 2017, https://www.nytimes.com/2017/11/25/us/ohio-hovater-white-nationalist.html.

FAUSSET, RICHARD, AND ALAN FEUER. "Far-Right Groups Surge Into National View in Charlottesville." *The New York Times*, 13 Aug. 2017, https://www.nytimes.com/2017/08/13/us/far-right-groups-blaze-into-national-view-in-charlottesville.html.

FAUSSET, RICHARD, ET AL. "A Year After Charlottesville, Disarray in the White Supremacist Movement." *The New York Times*, 13 Aug. 2018, https://www.nytimes.com/2018/08/13/us/charlottesville-unite-the-right-white-supremacists.html.

FEUER, ALAN. "Far Right Plans Its Next Moves With a New Energy." *The New York Times*, 14 Aug. 2017, https://www.nytimes.com/2017/08/14/us/white-supremacists-right-wing-extremists-richard-spencer.html.

GOLDSTEIN, JOSEPH. "Alt-Right Gathering Exults in Trump Election With Nazi-Era Salute." *The New York Times*, 20 Nov. 2016, https://www.nytimes.com/2016/11/21/us/alt-right-salutes-donald-trump.html.

HAKIM, DANNY, AND STEPHANIE SAUL. "White Nationalists Love Corey Stewart. He Keeps Them Close." *The New York Times*, 5 Aug. 2018, https://www.nytimes.com/2018/08/05/us/politics/corey-stewart-virginia.html.

HARMON, AMY. "Geneticists Criticize Use of Science by White Nationalists to Justify 'Racial Purity.' " *The New York Times*, 19 Oct. 2018, https://www.nytimes.com/2018/10/19/us/white-supremacists-science-genetics.html.

HARMON, AMY. "Why White Supremacists Are Chugging Milk (and Why Geneticists Are Alarmed)." *The New York Times*, 17 Oct. 2018, https://www.nytimes.com/2018/10/17/us/white-supremacists-science-dna.html.

HARTOCOLLIS, ANEMONA. "University of Florida Braces for Richard Spencer."

The New York Times, 17 Oct. 2017, https://www.nytimes.com/2017/10/17/us/florida-richard-spencer.html.

HAUSER, CHRISTINE. "After Neo-Nazi Posting, Police in Whitefish, Mont., Step Up Patrols." *The New York Times*, 20 Dec. 2016, https://www.nytimes.com/2016/12/20/us/whitefish-montana-jews-daily-stormer.html.

HESS, AMANDA. "The Far Right Has a New Digital Safe Space." *The New York Times*, 30 Nov. 2016, https://www.nytimes.com/2016/11/30/arts/the-far-right-has-a-new-digital-safe-space.html.

ISMAY, JOHN. "Rhodesia's Dead — but White Supremacists Have Given It New Life Online." *The New York Times*, 10 Apr. 2018, https://www.nytimes.com/2018/04/10/magazine/rhodesia-zimbabwe-white-supremacists.html.

JACOBS, JULIA. "Jury Recommends Life in Prison for James Fields in Fatal Charlottesville Attack." *The New York Times*, 11 Dec. 2018, https://www.nytimes.com/2018/12/11/us/james-fields-charlottesville-sentence.html.

JACOBS, JULIA. "White Supremacists' Use of Campus Propaganda Is Soaring, Report Finds." *The New York Times*, 28 June 2018, https://www.nytimes.com/2018/06/28/us/white-supremacist-groups-adl.html.

KELLY, ANNIE. "The Housewives of White Supremacy." *The New York Times*, 1 June 2018, https://www.nytimes.com/2018/06/01/opinion/sunday/tradwives-women-alt-right.html.

LACEY, MARC. "Readers Accuse Us of Normalizing a Nazi Sympathizer; We Respond." *The New York Times*, 26 Nov. 2017, https://www.nytimes.com/2017/11/26/reader-center/readers-accuse-us-of-normalizing-a-nazi-sympathizer-we-respond.html.

THE NEW YORK TIMES. " 'The Daily' Transcript: Interview With Former White Nationalist Derek Black." *The New York Times*, 22 Aug. 2017, https://www.nytimes.com/2017/08/22/podcasts/the-daily-transcript-derek-black.html.

THE NEW YORK TIMES. "Some Readers Say 'White Nationalist' Normalizes the Charlottesville Protesters." *The New York Times*, 14 Aug. 2017, https://www.nytimes.com/2017/08/14/reader-center/some-readers-say-white-nationalist-normalizes-the-charlottesville-protesters.html.

PERRY, ANDRE. "Why Squirrel Hill Is a Target for White Supremacists." *The New York Times*, 29 Oct. 2018, https://www.nytimes.com/2018/10/29/opinion/pittsburgh-squirrel-hill.html.

RAPPEPORT, ALAN, AND NOAH WEILAND. "White Nationalists Celebrate 'an Awakening' After Donald Trump's Victory." *The New York Times*, 19 Nov.

2016, https://www.nytimes.com/2016/11/20/us/politics/white-nationalists-celebrate-an-awakening-after-donald-trumps-victory.html.

ROBLES, FRANCES, ET AL. "Dylann Roof, Suspect in Charleston Shooting, Flew the Flags of White Power." *The New York Times*, 18 June 2015, https://www.nytimes.com/2015/06/19/us/on-facebook-dylann-roof-charleston-suspect-wears-symbols-of-white-supremacy.html.

ROOSE, KEVIN. "On Gab, an Extremist-Friendly Site, Pittsburgh Shooting Suspect Aired His Hatred in Full." *The New York Times*, 28 Oct. 2018, https://www.nytimes.com/2018/10/28/us/gab-robert-bowers-pittsburgh-synagogue-shootings.html.

ROOSE, KEVIN, AND ALI WINSTON. "Far-Right Internet Groups Listen for Trump's Approval, and Often Hear It." *The New York Times*, 4 Nov. 2018, https://www.nytimes.com/2018/11/04/us/politics/far-right-internet-trump.html.

SPENCER, HAWES, AND SHERYL GAY STOLBERG. "White Nationalists March on University of Virginia." *The New York Times*, 11 Aug. 2017, https://www.nytimes.com/2017/08/11/us/white-nationalists-rally-charlottesville-virginia.html.

STACK, LIAM. "Attack on Alt-Right Leader Has Internet Asking: Is It O.K. to Punch a Nazi?" *The New York Times*, 21 Jan. 2017, https://www.nytimes.com/2017/01/21/us/politics/richard-spencer-punched-attack.html.

STEVENS, MATT. "Christopher Cantwell, White Nationalist in Vice Video, Braces for Charges." *The New York Times*, 21 Aug. 2017, https://www.nytimes.com/2017/08/21/us/christopher-cantwell-charlottesville.html.

STOLBERG, SHERYL GAY, AND BRIAN M. ROSENTHAL. "Man Charged After White Nationalist Rally in Charlottesville Ends in Deadly Violence." *The New York Times*, 12 Aug. 2017, https://www.nytimes.com/2017/08/12/us/charlottesville-protest-white-nationalist.html.

TAUB, AMANDA. " 'White Nationalism,' Explained." *The New York Times*, 21 Nov. 2016, https://www.nytimes.com/2016/11/22/world/americas/white-nationalism-explained.html.

TAVERNISE, SABRINA. "Why the Announcement of a Looming White Minority Makes Demographers Nervous." *The New York Times*, 22 Nov. 2018, https://www.nytimes.com/2018/11/22/us/white-americans-minority-population.html.

THRUSH, GLENN, AND MAGGIE HABERMAN. "Trump Gives White Supremacists an Unequivocal Boost." *The New York Times*, 15 Aug. 2017, https://www

.nytimes.com/2017/08/15/us/politics/trump-charlottesville-white-nationalists.html.

VICTOR, DANIEL. "NPR Is Criticized After White Nationalist Ranks the Races by Intelligence on Air." *The New York Times*, 10 Aug. 2018, https://www.nytimes.com/2018/08/10/business/media/charlottesville-jason-kessler-npr.html.

WEILAND, NOAH. "Before 'Unite the Right' Rally, Trump Does Not Condemn Supremacists." *The New York Times*, 11 Aug. 2018, https://www.nytimes.com/2018/08/11/us/politics/unite-the-right-2018-dc-rally.html.

WEILAND, NOAH. "White Nationalist Richard Spencer Is Barred From Speaking at a Federal Building." *The New York Times*, 2 Nov. 2017, https://www.nytimes.com/2017/11/02/us/politics/richard-spencer-washington-conference.html.

WINES, MICHAEL, AND STEPHANIE SAUL. "White Supremacists Extend Their Reach Through Websites" *The New York Times*, 5 July 2015, https://www.nytimes.com/2015/07/06/us/white-supremacists-extend-their-reach-through-websites.html.

Index

This book is current up until the time of printing. For the most up-to-date reporting, visit www.nytimes.com.